D0338407

SHE TOPPLED FORWARD AND FELL HEADLONG DOWN
A STEEP FLIGHT OF STONE STEPS.

The Hidden Staircase. *Page* 150

A MAN CAME OUT OF THE HOUSE.

The Hidden Staircase. *Page* 130

SINGLE FILE, NANCY AND THE TWO LADIES TRUDGED UP THE NARROW STAIRS LEADING TO THE ATTIC.

The Hidden Staircase. *Page 73*

" AND THAT ISN'T THE WORST—LOOK UP THERE ! "

The Hidden Staircase. *Frontispiece* (*Page* 96)

NANCY DREW MYSTERY STORIES

THE HIDDEN STAIRCASE

By

CAROLYN KEENE

AUTHOR OF

NANCY DREW MYSTERY STORIES: THE SECRET OF THE OLD CLOCK

NANCY DREW MYSTERY STORIES: THE BUNGALOW MYSTERY

ILLUSTRATED BY

RUSSELL H. TANDY

WITH AN INTRODUCTION BY

NANCY PICKARD

FACSIMILE EDITION

1991

BEDFORD, MA

APPLEWOOD BOOKS

Distributed by The Globe Pequot Press

Chester, CT

ISBN: 1-55709-156-0

The Nancy Drew® Mystery Stories were originally published by Grosset & Dunlap, Inc. Applewood Books acknowledges their kind permission to reprint these books.

For further information about these editions please write:
Applewood Books, 18 North Road, Bedford, MA 01730.

First Printing

10 9 8 7 6 5 4 3 2 1

PUBLISHER'S NOTE

Applewood Books is pleased to reissue the original Hardy Boys and Nancy Drew books, just as they were originally published—the Hardy Boys in 1927 and Nancy Drew in 1930. In 1959, the books were condensed and rewritten, and since then, the original editions have been out of print.

Much has changed in America since the books were first issued. The modern reader may be delighted with the warmth and exactness of the language, the wholesome innocence of the characters, their engagement with the natural world, or the nonstop action without the use of violence; but just as well, the modern reader may be extremely uncomfortable with the racial and social stereotyping, the roles women play in these books, or the use of phrases or situations which may conjure up some response in the modern reader that was not felt by the reader of the times.

For good or bad, we Americans have changed quite a bit since these books were first issued. Many readers will remember these editions with great affection and will be delighted with their return; others will wonder why we just don't let them disappear. These books are part of our heritage. They are a window on our real past. For that reason, except for the addition of this note and the introduction by Nancy Pickard, we are presenting *The Hidden Staircase* unedited and unchanged from its first edition.

Applewood Books
September 1991

I OWE IT ALL TO NANCY DREW

By
NANCY PICKARD
AUTHOR OF
THE JENNY CAIN MYSTERY SERIES: GENEROUS DEATH
THE JENNY CAIN MYSTERY SERIES: BUM STEER
THE JENNY CAIN MYSTERY SERIES: I.O.U.
& OTHERS

WHEN I was ten years old, I wrote: "I will be happy if I can have horses, solve mysteries, help people, and be happily married." In that order. For thirty years after that, I forgot on any conscious level about that wish list. When I finally came across it again, I was forty years old, married to a cowboy, doing volunteer work, and writing murder mysteries.

The child was, indeed, the mother to this woman.

It's easy enough to figure out why I wanted to "have horses"—doesn't almost every adolescent girl dream of riding Black Beauty? Growing up in the '50s made it *de rigueur* for me to want to "be happily married," and being a college student in the '60s made it nearly obligatory for me to want to "help people." But whence the desire to "solve mysteries"?

That's easy, isn't it?

I read Nancy Drew. Didn't you?

Sometimes I think I owe it all to her—my career, my amateur sleuth heroine, most of whatever finer qualities I may possess, even my blond hair, blue eyes, and my name. Nancy Drew was (almost) everything I wanted to be when I grew up: intelligent, self-confident, incredibly courageous, honest, straightforward, kind, courteous, energetic, successful, and independent. I confess that I also wished I were well-to-do and beautiful, just like Nancy. Granted, it's possible that she could have used more of a sense of fun and humor, and it cannot be denied that in her language and attitudes she reflected the white, middle-class, Christian prejudices of her day, but I'd rather blame those failings on her creators. I like to think that had Nancy but known, she never would have thought, spoken, or behaved in those ways.

Recently, for the first time since I was a girl the original version of *The Hidden Staircase*, I read the story you now hold in your hands. First published in 1930, it may be the most famous and the most fondly remembered of any of the Nancy Drew mysteries. In 1959 the story was republished in a rewritten edition that drastically altered both the plot and the characters. If I had a daughter, this original version is the one I'd want to pass on to her. It is the edition I will give to my son.

I think it is not overstating the case to maintain that the original Nancy Drew is a mythic character in the psyches of the American women who followed her adventures as they were growing up. She may have been Superman, Batman, and Green Hornet, all wrapped up in a pretty girl in a blue convertible.

This original *Hidden Staircase* is a rich and nutritious feast of psychological archetypes, so that it assumes the quality of fairy tale and myth. Nancy herself, in this version, is quite a heroic figure, one that in our culture we're more accustomed to seeing portrayed as a boy than as a girl: she's incorruptibly honest, steadfast, and courageous, a veritable Sir Lancelot of a girl, off on a quest to rescue the fair maiden who is, in this case, her father, and to recapture the holy grail, which is in this case a silver spoon, a pocketbook, a diamond pin and a couple of black silk dresses.

We'd have to go back to ancient goddess mythology to find an equivalent female of such heroic stature, back to a figure such as Innana, who was the chief Sumerian deity, a woman who went to hell and back on a rescue mission. Such journeys into the "underground" are viewed in psychological terms as descents into one's unconscious; it is believed that a person must bring the contents of the unconscious into the light of consciousness in order to fully integrate one's psyche. In *The Hidden Staircase*, Nancy symbolically does just that, by tumbling like Alice down a black hole and then by journeying deeper and deeper into a really quite frightening tunnel where she perseveres with remarkable courage until she finds a way to ascend once more into the light. In so doing, she solves all mysteries and reunites everyone and everything that have been wrongfully separated. This is, at heart, no "mere" adventure story; this is myth.

In this original story, Nancy works alone, facing every terror on her own, although with the support, encouragement, and appreciation of the grown-ups. It reminds me of mythic initiation rites, where the young person is challenged, with the full backing of the adults, to prove herself. Nancy's father, in this version, is an ideally archetypal figure who approves of everything his daughter does and praises her unstintingly. He's so proud of her he could bust, as proud as fathers are said to be when their sons make the winning touchdown in a football game, as proud as Zeus was of Athena. In this version, Nancy is a marvel of decisiveness and resolution, and she gets to experience a full personal triumph.

Do you remember how you felt when you read this story?

I remember exactly how it was for me....

I was scared and had gooseflesh, and my stomach clenched, and the hair on my arms stood on end, and I tucked my feet beneath me so the boogieman under the bed couldn't grab them, and when Nancy was in the tunnel I could hardly bear to turn the page for fear of what might happen next, and yet I couldn't help turning the page to see what happened next. Oh, it was wonderful! It was delicious. It was spooky and mysterious and creepy, and I was there falling down those stairs with her, praying the flashlight wouldn't go out, feeling my way along the dark, damp walls of the tunnel, almost plunging through the wood where the stair was missing, breathing a sigh of vast relief when Nancy pulled the iron ring and the other door opened....

All of that is still here.

The faults are still here, too—the racism and anti-Semitism—and they make for painful reading now, just as they did for their victims back then. I hope they'll inspire us to examine our own "historical context" for the prejudices we don't know we have.

Do you want to know another truth? I miss her.

I miss the sheer joy of reading a "Nancy Drew."

Evidently millions of other women do, too, because they're turning in record numbers to read the new breed of adult fictional women sleuths whose undeniable progenitor is Nancy Drew. It is surely no coincidence that my own detective, Jenny Cain, has a name that matched Nancy's syllable for syllable, and that she's slim, blond, and blue-eyed, too. My Jenny is as good as motherless, like Nancy, and she's smarter, braver, and more resourceful than her own father, like Nancy. More than one reviewer has referred to her as "Nancy Drew all grown up," which I take as truth and compliment.

The real Nancy Drew mystery may be the Mystery of the Appeal of Nancy Drew herself, and of her phenomenal attraction to successive generations of American girls.

I believe the solution to that mystery is this...

Nancy Drew, especially the Nancy of this original

story, is our bright heroine, chasing down the shadows, conquering our worst fears, giving us a glimpse of our brave and better selves, proving to everybody exactly how admirable and wonderful a thing it is to be a girl.

Thank you, Nancy Drew.

NANCY DREW MYSTERY STORIES

THE HIDDEN STAIRCASE

BY

CAROLYN KEENE

AUTHOR OF "THE SECRET OF THE OLD CLOCK," "THE BUNGALOW MYSTERY," ETC.

ILLUSTRATED BY

RUSSELL H. TANDY

NEW YORK

GROSSET & DUNLAP

PUBLISHERS

Made in the United States of America

NANCY DREW MYSTERY STORIES

By CAROLYN KEENE

12mo. Cloth. Illustrated.

THE SECRET OF THE OLD CLOCK

THE HIDDEN STAIRCASE

THE BUNGALOW MYSTERY

(Other volumes in preparation)

GROSSET & DUNLAP, PUBLISHERS, NEW YORK

CONTENTS

Contents

THE HIDDEN STAIRCASE

CHAPTER I

A Rude Visitor

"I declare, I don't know what makes me so nervous this afternoon! I have the strangest feeling—just as though something were about to happen."

As Nancy Drew expressed the thought aloud, she tossed aside a book she had been trying to read and restlessly crossed the living room to glance out of the window. She was alone in the big house, for her father, Carson Drew, had been called out of the city on an important law case and Hannah Gruen, the housekeeper, had taken her day off.

Usually, Nancy enjoyed a book, but on this particular afternoon she had been unable to interest herself in anything. For no apparent reason she felt nervous and uneasy.

As she stood at the window, her eyes rested for a moment upon an old-fashioned mantel clock above the fireplace. The timepiece aroused pleasant memories, for it had been given to her as a reward for her service in solving a baffling mystery. Nancy smiled.

"I know what's the matter with me," she told herself. "I'm aching for another adventure. That's all the good it will do me, too!"

With a sigh of resignation, she again settled herself in a comfortable chair and took up her book. She had read scarcely a page when her attention was attracted by the sound of a heavy step on the front veranda.

The doorbell rang sharply. There was an electric something about the ring which was arresting, startling. Before Nancy could get up from the chair, the bell rang a second time.

She dropped her book and hurried to the door. Opening it, she stood face to face with a man she had never seen before.

He was unusually tall and thin with spindling legs which gave him the appearance of a towering scarecrow. The illusion was heightened by his clothing, which was ill-fitting and several seasons out of style. Nancy could not help but notice several grease spots on his coat. However, it was not the man's clothing or miserly appearance which repulsed her, but rather his unpleasant face. He had sharp, piercing eyes which seemed to bore into her.

Nancy was permitted but an instant to appraise her visitor, for as she opened the door he stepped inside without waiting for an invitation. This rude action somewhat nonplused her, but she was too polite to show her displeasure.

"I am Nathan Gombet of Cliffwood," the man told her bluntly. "I want to see Carson Drew."

"My father isn't here now," Nancy explained quietly.

"Where is he?"

Nancy did not like the brusque way Nathan Gombet had of asking questions, but she answered him politely.

"Out of town on business."

"But I must see him."

"I'm very sorry," Nancy returned patiently, "but it is impossible. He won't be back until late this evening. If you will come back to-morrow——"

"To-morrow won't do. I want to see him now," he demanded.

"Can't you understand that my father is out of town?" Nancy asked a trifle tartly, for she was beginning to be irritated. "If you want to leave a message, I'll give it to him as soon as he comes in."

"I don't want to leave a message. I came

after those papers. Did your father leave them for me?"

"I don't know what papers you mean."

"Oh, you don't, eh? Well, your father knows all right. Just ask him about Nathan Gombet's property rights on the river and he'll tell you all about the nasty deal he and his friends tried to slip over on me!"

"What are you talking about?" Nancy demanded sharply. "Have you lost your senses?"

"I've just come to 'em, that's what I've done. Maybe you don't know about it, but I own some property down along the river. Your father induced me to sell a piece of it at a ridiculously low figure. The land is worth several times what he paid me for it. I'm not going to let anyone put over a raw deal like that. I want the deed back or my price, and Carson Drew is going to give it to me, too!"

"You don't know what you are saying," Nancy said icily. "My father wouldn't cheat anyone out of a cent."

"Oh, no!" Nathan exclaimed sarcastically. "I suppose he's in business for his health!"

"He's not in the business of taking what doesn't belong to him—that's certain!" Nancy retorted hotly. "If you have anything coming to you I'm sure it will be turned over to you just as soon as my father returns."

"Just as soon as he returns—that's good," Nathan sneered. "Like as not he's hiding somewhere in the house this very minute."

"How dare you insinuate such a thing?" Nancy cried angrily. "I'm alone in the house."

The instant she had divulged the information, she could have bitten her tongue.

"Alone, eh? Well, maybe I was mistaken about your father being here, but it's the truth I've been telling you about those papers. He cheated me out of a pile of money."

"It isn't the truth, and you know it! I've listened to you just as long as I intend to. You ought to be ashamed to come here and say such insulting things about my father. Now I wish you'd go!"

"I'll not stir until I get my papers!"

"I've told you I don't know a thing about your old papers."

"They're here some place. I know they're in the house."

"Will you kindly leave?"

"Just try to put me out if you think you can!" Nathan Gombet said, with an unpleasant leer. "You know more about those papers than you let on."

"You're crazy!" Nancy snapped. She was so exasperated that she could not keep her temper in check.

Nathan Gombet's eyes narrowed to mere slits and a cruel look came over his face.

"Get those papers for me!" he commanded harshly.

Nancy was aware that her father sometimes kept valuable papers in his desk, but she had no intention of handing over any of them to this man. She had never heard her father mention the documents in question, but she had no doubt that Gombet was trying to get something which did not belong to him. Although frightened at the man's strange conduct, she faced him boldly.

"I'll not give you anything! Now get out of here!"

"All right, if you'll not hand over the papers, I'll just have a look around for myself."

A crafty look had come into the man's eyes. As he spoke, he moved toward the study which adjoined the living room. From where he had been standing, Carson Drew's desk was in plain sight.

"Don't you dare go in there!" Nancy cried indignantly.

"Oh, so that's where the papers are? I thought as much!"

A half dozen long strides took Nathan Gombet across the room and into the study. Reaching the desk he jerked open a drawer and began pawing through it.

"Stop that!" Angrily, Nancy grasped the man by the coat and pulled him away from the desk. "You get out of here or I'll call the police!"

With one vicious jerk, Nathan Gombet freed himself and wheeled upon her. His face was convulsed with rage and Nancy saw that he was desperate.

Instinctively, she threw up her hands to ward off a blow.

CHAPTER II

A Warning of Trouble

Nathan Gombet did not strike Nancy Drew, although for an instant it appeared that he intended to do so. He remained motionless, regarding her with a hatred he made no effort to conceal. His face was distorted and he stood in a half-crouched position, like an animal about to pounce upon its prey.

Nancy knew that she must act quickly, for she saw the man was beside himself with rage. Unless she handed over the papers he demanded, she did not doubt but that he would attempt to do her bodily injury. She must depend upon her own wits to save her, for there was no one within calling distance. If only she could reach the telephone!

As the thought came to her, her eyes rested for a moment on the instrument. Nathan Gombet saw the look and understood that she intended to carry out her threat to telephone the authorities. His lips parted in an ugly snarl.

"Call the police, will you? Oh, no, my little lady, you won't do that!"

He made a vicious lunge for her, but she was too quick for him. As he reached out to grab her, she stepped to one side and, neatly eluding his clawlike hands, placed the table between them. She caught up the telephone receiver.

Gombet saw that Nancy Drew was not to be bluffed and instantly a change came over him. The look of anger on his face changed to one of genuine fear.

"Don't telephone," he begged almost childishly. "I'll go."

Nancy hesitated, undecided in her course. She had no wish to start a scandal in River Heights by calling the attention of the police to the threats the man had made, for she realized that the resulting publicity might not do her father any good. Yet she wondered if she could trust the man to keep his word.

"All right, then, go," she said curtly, without relinquishing her hold on the telephone. "I'll give you twenty seconds to get out of here! If I see you hanging around the house I'll call the police!"

Hastily, Nathan Gombet picked up his hat and with a last glance toward Carson Drew's desk, turned to leave. Nancy followed him from the study, watching him closely lest he try to work a trick upon her.

In the doorway, the man paused and looked back.

"I'll have my rights before I get through," he muttered. "Your father ain't seen the last o' this, not by a jugful!"

Slamming the door behind him, he tramped across the porch and was gone. From the living room window Nancy watched him until he disappeared beyond the corner.

"I almost wish I'd called the police," she thought. "The idea of saying the things he did about Dad! He thought he could scare me into giving him those papers!"

The encounter had disturbed her considerably, for she realized that in Nathan Gombet her father could have a troublesome enemy. She was convinced that the man was without scruples. Unquestionably, his accusations were entirely false, but if he spread his story about River Heights, undiscerning persons might accept it as fact.

As former district attorney at River Heights, a city in the Middle West, Carson Drew had built up an enviable reputation for himself, but the character of his work was such that he had made enemies as well as staunch friends. Those whom he had antagonized were ever on the lookout for an opportunity to undermine the reputation he had made for himself. So far, Carson Drew had more than held his own against unscrupulous persons, for he was known as a "fighter."

Nancy was Carson Drew's only child, but, though she had been indulged, she had never been spoiled. She was an unusually pretty girl, fair of skin with friendly blue eyes and golden curly hair. Her friends declared that she was as clever as she was attractive.

Since the death of her mother a number of years before, Nancy had found it necessary to be resourceful and efficient. Not only had she assumed the management of the Drew household, but she took a keen interest in her father's law cases, especially those which smacked of mystery. She had been present at a number of interviews with noted detectives, and her father declared she had a natural talent for digging into interesting cases.

Only the summer before, she had taken it upon her own slender shoulders to solve a mystery which had baffled capable lawyers. When no one could locate Josiah Crowley's missing will, Nancy, in an effort to aid Abigail Rowen and Allie and Grace Horner, had taken over the task herself. Her thrilling adventures, which included an encounter with robbers, are told in that first volume of this series, entitled, "The Secret of the Old Clock."

Of late, Nancy Drew had longed for another exciting experience which would give her an opportunity to use her wits, little dreaming of what was in store for her.

Yet, as she turned slowly away from the window after watching Nathan Gombet vanish down the street, she had a certain premonition of trouble ahead.

"If I hadn't threatened to call the police, that man would have injured me," she thought. "I do wish father were here. I want to tell him about Nathan Gombet and the threat he made. It wouldn't surprise me if he should try to make trouble."

Nancy was indeed disturbed. Never for an instant did she credit any of the statements the man had made, but from his appearance and actions, she was inclined to believe that he would stoop to anything in order to gain his end.

"He has some dishonest scheme up his sleeve," she assured herself. "Dad will explain everything when he comes home."

Try as she would, she could not forget the unpleasant interview. Her afternoon was completely ruined. In vain she tried to read. After a time she busied herself with some sewing, but had to rip nearly everything out.

"It's no use," she sighed. "I can't keep my mind on what I'm doing. I wish someone would come home. This house is getting on my nerves!"

Glancing at the clock, Nancy saw that it was only four o'clock. Hannah would not return for at least an hour, and she could not expect her father until late that evening. Folding up her sewing, she arose and crossed over to the desk. She regarded it speculatively.

"Gombet said it was a deed he wanted," she told herself. "If it's actually here I think I'd better find it and put it in the safe."

She seated herself before the desk and, opening a drawer, began to go over the papers carefully. As she examined the first document she picked up, there came a sharp ring of the doorbell.

So unexpected was the noise that Nancy started. What could it mean? Had Nathan Gombet returned to make more trouble?

Quickly thrusting the papers back into the desk, she closed down the top and locked it. Then she made her way resolutely to the front door.

CHAPTER III

Interesting Information

Nancy Drew swung open the heavy oak door, fully expecting to see Nathan Gombet on the veranda. She had braced herself for another unpleasant ordeal, but when she saw that her fears were groundless, her face relaxed into a pleased smile.

"Allie Horner!" she exclaimed enthusiastically. "What a scare you gave me!"

"Meaning that I look a fright?" Allie bantered.

"Mercy, no! I can't remember that I ever saw you looking better in your life."

The compliment was a sincere one. In the last few months plenty of good food and freedom from worry had done wonders for Allie. She had grown becomingly plump and there were roses in her cheeks. Her eyes were bright and she seemed to have an overabundance of vitality.

Nancy could remember the day when she first met Allie Horner and her sister, Grace. They lived on a farm along the River Road and at the time were undernourished and beset with financial worries. Through Nancy's efforts, the girls had come into an inheritance, and their troubles had vanished. They still resided on the River Road, but they had used a portion of their income to modernize the place, with the result that it was considered a model farm.

"Do come into the living room, Allie," Nancy urged cordially. "It's been months since I saw you last."

"Grace and I don't get to town very often."

"Too busy, I suppose. But I'm so glad you came to-day. I've been lonesome for someone to talk with."

"I can't stay very long, Nancy. I dropped in to give you a little present."

"A present?"

"Yes, it's not much of a gift, I'm afraid," Allie smiled apologetically as she thrust two packages into Nancy's hands. "Just a chicken for your Sunday dinner and two dozen eggs."

"Why, that's a fine gift, Allie! You're never sure of getting fresh eggs when you buy them at the grocery store—you have to take the fresh part on trust. And sometimes your trust is betrayed."

"I think you'll find these eggs fresh. I gathered them this morning."

After thanking Allie for the gift, Nancy carried the chicken and the eggs to the kitchen and placed them in the electrical refrigerator. Returning to the living room, she pulled her chair up close to Allie's, and the two girls settled themselves for a chat.

"Tell me about everything," Nancy commanded. "How is your sister?"

"Oh, Grace is fine, and fairly rolling in wealth," Allie declared proudly. "She wanted to come with me this afternoon, but she couldn't take the time from her work. Dressmaking has picked up tremendously and she has more orders than she can fill. You should see her new electric sewing machine."

"I suppose you've made a great many changes since I last visited your place?"

"Oh, yes. We get a big kick out of landscaping everything. We've even gone in for grand names—we call our place the chicken ranch now. I've had wonderful luck with my Leghorns, and I intend to double my flock next year."

As Allie spoke, her eyes came to rest upon the old-fashioned mantel clock.

"Every time I see that old clock I think of how much you did for all of us," she said quietly to Nancy. "I wish you would permit Grace and me to give you a more suitable reward."

"But the clock is all I want, really it is," Nancy protested.

"You're the strangest girl I ever knew," Allie sighed. "Oh, well, I know it won't do any good to urge you, so I'll drop the matter. Tell me about yourself."

"There's nothing to tell."

"Then you're not involved in any more mysteries?"

"Not so far as I know," Nancy laughed. Then the smile faded from her face and she regarded Allie seriously. "Still, an odd thing did happen this afternoon, just a few minutes before you arrived."

"Tell me about it."

"Well, a strange man came to the door and asked to see my father. When I told him Dad was out of town on important business he didn't believe me. He ranted a lot about his 'property rights on the river,' whatever that may mean. He claimed that he had been cheated out of some money. If I hadn't threatened to call the police he would have gone through everything in Dad's desk."

"You have no idea who the man was?"

"I never saw him before, but he gave his name as Nathan Gombet."

"Nathan Gombet?"

"Yes, do you know him?"

"Well, rather! He used to buy eggs and

chickens from me until I told him not to come back any more. He's a regular miser, if ever there was one. He has a home over in Cliffwood."

"I suspected he was a miser from his appearance."

"You can't trust him out of your sight. One day after I had sold him five dozen eggs I turned my back for a minute and he tried to slip an extra dozen into the crate!"

"He claims my father cheated him out of his property rights."

Allie laughed shortly.

"Knowing Nathan as I do, I'd be quicker to think he was trying to cheat your father. What property does he mean?"

"I don't know anything about it except that it's along the river."

"It must be the property that was condemned for the railroad bridge," Allie suggested.

"Did the bridge go up on Gombet's land?"

"As I recall it, he sold a strip of land on either side of the river. Then after the bridge went up he claimed the railroad had built over its boundary line."

"Why didn't he find that out before the bridge was finished?"

"Oh, no one believes his claim, Nancy. The land was carefully surveyed, you know. It's my personal opinion Nathan Gombet isn't perfectly right in his mind."

"You mean he's——"

"Oh, I wouldn't go so far as to say he's crazy, Nancy; but he's money mad. It's an obsession with him that someone is trying to cheat him out of something. He went nearly daffy when the bridge went up. He even threatened he'd blow it up if they didn't pay him his price."

"He ought to be arrested. It's dangerous to have him at large."

"Yes, I think so myself. Of course it's only a rumor about his threat to blow up the bridge, but I believe he said it all right."

"So do I, after the way he acted this afternoon. He'll bear watching."

Allie nodded soberly.

"You're going to tell your father, aren't you?" Allie queried.

"Oh, yes, just as soon as he gets home."

The girls talked for some time and then Allie Horner announced that she must leave.

"I have a notion to ride out into the country with you and hike back," Nancy told her. "Father won't be back for several hours yet and I'm tired of sitting here in the house with nothing to do."

"I wish you would come with me," Allie urged.

"All right. Wait until I get my hiking boots and I'll do it!"

Nancy left the room and soon returned dressed for hiking. After locking the doors and windows, she left the house with Allie.

"How do you like our new automobile?" Allie demanded, as she paused in front of a roadster which was parked at the curbing. "Grace and I bought it last week."

"It's a beauty," Nancy replied. "You didn't tell me about that."

"I intended to, but we got to talking about Nathan Gombet and I forgot."

The two girls sprang into the roadster and Allie took the wheel. She drove rather slowly, for as yet she was not perfectly familiar with the various controls.

When they came to the Muskoka River Nancy thanked Allie for the ride, and expressed the intention of hiking back.

"If I walk right along, I'll get home before dark," she assured Allie, as she stepped from the roadster.

Nancy Drew watched Allie out of sight, and then struck off at a brisk pace along the river.

"A walk will do me good," she told herself. "It may help me get rid of my nervousness."

Although the day was warm, there was a cool breeze blowing along the river, and Nancy found the air invigorating. She swung blithely along, pausing occasionally to skip a tiny stone out into the water or to watch a school of minnows in the shallows near shore.

After a time, the path led through thick bushes and tall trees. When she emerged into the clearing again she saw, less than three hundred yards ahead of her, a gigantic arc of iron and steel that stretched across the Muskoka River. It was the first time Nancy had ever seen the new railroad bridge at close range and she gave a cry of interest.

Hurrying on, she climbed over a fence which marked the boundary of the railroad right of way and came to the tracks. There she paused and surveyed the bridge with awe.

"It must have cost a mint of money," she thought.

As she was considering the remarkable engineering feat which the bridge represented, a shrill locomotive whistle caused her to wheel about. The block signal was down and she knew a train was approaching from the west.

She moved hastily to a safe distance from the tracks. With a fascination which was tinged with horror, she watched a long, heavy eastbound flyer as it roared around the bend and like a mighty monster charged down upon the railroad bridge.

"What if Nathan Gombet dared to carry out his threat?" she asked herself, with a shudder.

Even after the flyer had clattered safely across the bridge and had vanished in a cloud of smoke, Nancy could not shake off the uneasy feeling which had taken possession of her.

Now that she had viewed the bridge, she had a graphic picture in her mind of the damage Gombet could accomplish if he were so inclined. As she turned away and walked slowly on toward her home, she lost herself in sober reflection.

"Nathan Gombet is a dangerous man, that's certain," she told herself. "If only there were some way to put him behind prison bars before he harms anyone!"

CHAPTER IV

A Second Call

It was nearly six o'clock when Nancy Drew reached home after her long tramp. She ate dinner and then waited impatiently for the arrival of her father on the evening train. At last she heard his step on the veranda and ran to meet him.

"Well, Nancy, how did you make out while I was gone?" Carson Drew asked, as he dropped his brief case on the table. "Everything go all right?"

"Oh, Dad, the meanest old man came to see you."

Quickly, Nancy poured out the story of her encounter with Nathan Gombet. Her father listened gravely until she had finished.

"So he came here to bother you, did he? I'm sorry you've worried so much about it. Next time don't let him in."

"But, Dad, there's nothing to what he says, is there? You don't owe him any money?"

"Not a cent, Nancy."

"That's what I thought. But why did he make such a fuss?"

"Because he's a natural trouble-maker, I guess. You see, some time ago Gombet's land was condemned for the railroad right of way. I was on the land commission and I saw to it that Gombet was well paid. He seemed satisfied with the deal which was made. But after the bridge went up he began to pester the commission for more money. Claimed that the bridge had damaged the rest of his property, and I don't know what all. I didn't pay much attention to his claims because they were ridiculous. He's only a sorehead."

"He's been making some ugly threats, Dad. It's said he talks about blowing up the bridge."

"A man in his right mind wouldn't go around telling things like that," Mr. Drew said, with a troubled frown. "I think I'd better keep an eye on him."

"You'll be careful, won't you, Dad?" Nancy pleaded. "I'm sure he means to do you harm."

"Yes, I'll be cautious," Carson Drew promised smilingly. "But I'm not afraid of Nathan Gombet. I know how to handle him. What worries me is the way he came here bothering you. If he should ever try to harm you——"

"Oh, I'll probably never see him again," Nancy said lightly. "At least I hope I never shall."

As she spoke, her eyes turned toward the window and what she saw caused them to dilate in horror.

"Oh," she gasped. "There was someone at the window just then! I saw the face distinctly! It was Nathan Gombet!"

"You must be mistaken," Carson Drew protested, as he too glanced toward the window.

"No, I'm sure of it, Dad. There's someone on the porch now."

Even at that moment there came a sharp rap on the door.

"Don't go," Nancy whispered. "I know it's Nathan Gombet and I believe he means to harm you. He may have a gun."

"I may as well see him now and get it over with, Nancy. I'll not have him snooping around here!"

Resolutely, Carson Drew walked to the front door and flung it open. The light from the living room revealed Nathan Gombet.

"Well?" Carson Drew demanded. "What do you want here?"

"You know what I want."

"What you want and what you may get are two entirely different matters. Come in. I have something to say to you."

Mr. Drew permitted the man to enter, but did not offer him a chair. He looked Nathan Gombet straight in the face, but the man could not return the straightforward gaze. Involuntarily, he lowered his eyes.

"Tell me what you mean by coming here and bothering my daughter?" Mr. Drew asked curtly.

"I came after my just due."

"Let me tell you something. If you bother Nancy again I'll turn you over to the police. Get that straight!"

"I want my rights."

"Your rights? What do you mean by rights? You've had more now than you deserve."

"You cheated me! My land was worth several times what I was paid for it. Either I want the deed back or I want my price."

"So you were trying to get the deed when you rumaged in my desk this afternoon?" Mr. Drew demanded severely. "Well, Nathan Gombet, it won't do you a particle of good if you do get your hands on it."

"What do you mean?"

"It has been recorded."

"Then I want my price."

"Why, you're crazy, man," Carson Drew snapped, with growing impatience; "the commission gave you your price once, and an exorbitant one it was, too! If the railroad hadn't wanted your land you couldn't have sold it for a dime."

"The railroad had to have my land. I could have had anything I wanted to ask."

"You're mistaken, Mr. Gombet. Charging all the traffic will bear doesn't go any more. Anyway, the bridge could have gone across the river at a point south of your land without costing the railroad a cent more money. You were lucky that they bought your property at any price."

"The bridge damaged the rest of my land."

"Damaged it?" Carson Drew smiled. "In what way?"

"Well, ah—" Nathan Gombet began to stammer. Then he thought of something. "The trains scare my horses."

"How many horses have you?"

"Why—er—one."

"Oh! You have one horses?" Mr. Drew smiled broadly and Nancy could not hold back a giggle.

"Don't you dare ridicule me!" Gombet snorted.

"I am not ridiculing you, Mr. Gombet. I am merely trying to bring you to reason. If I recall correctly, your horse is an old nag that couldn't even bat an eye at a train. At all events, your fight is with the railroad and not with me."

"You drew up the papers."

"I was merely acting as an agent."

"I don't care what you say. I know you and

your scheming friends are trying to swindle me out of my property!"

"I don't know how you came by such a silly idea. The land commission is very fair in all their dealings. What you ask is most unreasonable. As far as I am concerned, the matter is closed!"

"Not much it ain't! I was swindled out of ten thousand dollars!"

Carson Drew laughed shortly.

"It is useless for us to talk further, I see. I am convinced you are trying to work a graft, but you've come to the wrong place this time!"

"If you don't give me my money I'll——"

"None of your threats!" Mr. Drew cut him off sharply. "Now get out of here!"

"Give me my money."

"Not a cent."

"That's final?"

"Absolutely."

Nathan Gombet faced Carson Drew with clenched fists and his features were distorted by rage. Nancy, who stood a short distance away, was fearful lest he attack her father. But Mr. Drew showed no signs of flinching, and Gombet was not overburdened with courage. He preferred to obtain his ends by underhand methods.

He turned abruptly toward the door, but before he reached it he wheeled upon Carson

Drew again. Nancy thought that he looked like a wild animal making its last stand.

"Take warning, Carson Drew," he muttered. "If I don't get my money, I'll do something desperate!"

With that he slammed the door and vanished into the night.

"Oh, Dad, what did he mean by that?" Nancy cried, as soon as the door had closed behind the man. "I'm afraid he'll do something terrible —perhaps blow up the railroad bridge."

"I don't believe he'd dare attempt that, Nancy. Nathan Gombet isn't a very courageous man."

"Then he'll try something underhanded. I know he will!"

"You may be right about that, Nancy. He's obsessed with an idea, and there's no talking him out of it."

"An idea! I'd call it a mania!"

"Perhaps that's a better word to describe his state of mind."

"I'm afraid he'll try to harm you, Dad."

"I'm not afraid of him, Nancy."

"I know you're not, but he's a tricky sort of enemy to have. Promise me you'll be careful, won't you?"

"I'll promise, Nancy. Now, don't worry about it any more. Nothing will come of the threat, I am sure."

Mr. Drew picked up the evening paper and began to read as unconcernedly as though nothing had happened. Nancy found it impossible to follow her father's example. She was dreadfully worried, for she was afraid her father did not consider Nathan Gombet seriously. Oh, how she did hope he would be cautious!

CHAPTER V

Strange Happenings

With the passing days, nothing more was heard of Nathan Gombet, and Nancy Drew began to grow easier in her mind. After all, his threat had been nothing more than bluff, she assured herself. Probably she would never see him again.

But as she became less vigilant, she could not know that Nathan Gombet was plotting revenge. Happy in her false security, Nancy forgot about the man and turned her thoughts into more pleasant channels.

"I believe I'll call on Abigail Rowen this afternoon," she told her father one day at the luncheon table. "I haven't seen her for months and I'm curious to know how she is getting along."

"You'll be back before dark?"

"Oh, yes, I'll be gone only a few hours."

As soon as luncheon was over, Nancy backed her blue roadster from the double garage and set off for Abigail Rowen's cottage, which was several miles from River Heights.

Approaching the house, she was pleased to observe that there had been many changes in the last few months. The former description of the place, "the worst looking house on the road," no longer applied.

The cottage had received a fresh coat of white paint and the shutters were a gay green. The old picket fence had been torn entirely away, as had the old plank walk which led to the house. In its place there was a new one of concrete. The yard was well kept, and at the rear of the cottage Nancy saw a man working in a vegetable garden.

"I hope I'll find Abigail well," she thought, as she parked her roadster and walked toward the house.

She rapped firmly upon the door. As she waited for someone to answer the knock she could not help but recall the first time she had called upon Abigail Rowen. The old woman had been confined to her bed with injuries received from a bad fall, and Nancy had found her in a deplorable condition. There was little food or money with which to buy it, and Abigail had firmly refused medical attention because she could not pay for it.

It was through Nancy's instigation that she had received her inheritance from the Crowley estate and she had wisely devoted a portion of the money to medical service.

Nancy's thoughts were cut short as the door was opened by an old woman in a black silk dress. It was Abigail Rowen, and she beamed when she saw her visitor.

"Well, I declare, if it isn't Nancy Drew!" she exclaimed, with evident pleasure. "Do come in and sit a spell."

"How is your hip now?" Nancy inquired solicitously, as she followed Miss Rowen.

"It ain't hurt me for going on two months now. I still limp a bit, but the doctor says I'll soon get over that."

"You're looking much better than when I saw you last."

"And I'm feeling better too. Things looked mighty black for a while and I didn't much care whether I lived or died. I owe everything to you."

"Oh, not at all," Nancy said quickly.

As she entered the living room she saw that Abigail had another visitor.

"Rosemary, we were just speaking about Nancy Drew," Miss Rowen said by way of introduction. "Well, here she is. One of the finest girls you ever set eyes on." The old woman turned to Nancy. "I want you to meet my friend, Rosemary Turnbull. She came over from Cliffwood to see me to-day."

Graciously, Nancy acknowledged the introduction. Rosemary Turnbull was an elderly maiden lady, tall and a trifle too thin, but not at all severe-looking in spite of her clothing. She wore an old-fashioned dress, long and wide of skirt and high in the neck, but she had a kind face, and Nancy was instantly attracted to her.

"Nancy is just the girl to help you out of your difficulties, Rosemary," Abigail said significantly. "She helped me get my inheritance and I know she'll help you if you ask her."

"Certainly, I'll help anyone I can," Nancy agreed pleasantly. "What is it?"

"Well, I hardly know how to tell you," Rosemary Turnbull began. She laughed unsteadily. "It seems I'm living in a haunted house."

"A haunted house?" Nancy cried.

"Well, of course it isn't really haunted. I don't believe in ghosts and things like that." She lowered her voice. "But the strangest things have been happening lately."

"What sort of things?" Nancy asked, with interest.

"Mostly little things. But after a while they get on your nerves. You see, I live in an old stone house in Cliffwood——"

"Alone?" Nancy interrupted.

"Oh, no. My twin sister Floretta lives with me. Our house, which is generally known as The Mansion, was built before civil war time, so you can imagine how old it is." She laughed nervously. "A wonderful setting for a ghost story, isn't it?"

"Go on," Nancy begged.

"Floretta and I have lived there for thirty years and we've never been disturbed until recently. Just the last few weeks things have happened which we can't explain. We hear strange noises at night."

"In the attic?"

"Not exactly. We hear sounds in all parts of the house."

"You're sure it isn't mice?"

"Oh, mercy, it couldn't be mice or rats." Rosemary was horrified at the thought. "Floretta and I are very particular about anything like that. There isn't a mouse in our house."

"Tell her about the flies," Abigail prompted.

"Our house is just filled with them now," Rosemary declared. "And until lately we never had them at all. I can't understand it."

"So far your trouble doesn't sound very alarming," and Nancy smiled. "Probably there is a screen off some place."

Rosemary shook her head firmly.

"We thought the same, so we made a thorough inspection. And we're very particular to keep the doors and windows closed."

"Tell her about the shadows," Abigail encouraged.

"We see strange shadows on the walls,"

Rosemary went on. A note of fear had crept into her voice now.

"What sort of shadows?"

"Floretta thought she saw a human shadow one night. She's beginning to think the place is haunted. I don't put any stock in that theory, but I'll admit things are beginning to get on my nerves."

"That would be enough to get on anyone's nerves." Nancy was sympathetic.

"And music! One night only last week I distinctly heard someone playing on a stringed instrument. It was enough to set my teeth on edge. Floretta says she'll be a nervous wreck if she stays in the house another week. She didn't want me to leave her alone even for a few hours this afternoon. She wants me to consent to sell the house."

"And you don't wish to do that?"

"No. The Mansion has been in the Turnbull family for decades and you can't blame me for not wanting to turn it over to a stranger. I don't take much stock in ghosts and the like. I can't believe the house is haunted."

"Tell her about the spoon," Abigail prompted.

"There isn't anything particular to tell. One morning we found a silver spoon missing."

"Are you sure it couldn't have been misplaced?" Nancy inquired.

"Floretta and I searched everywhere. We didn't think so much about it until we missed the pocketbook."

"You lost a pocketbook, too?"

"Yes. Only yesterday morning we discovered a purse was missing."

"This begins to look serious. Was there anything of value in it?"

"Nothing except a little money. Eight dollars and fourteen cents, as I remember."

"You keep no servants?"

"Floretta and I have done our own work for years. We have a man to take care of the yard."

"How long has he been in your employ?"

"Oh, for eight or ten years. He's perfectly honest. We know he wouldn't touch a thing."

"Have you noticed any prowlers about the house?" Nancy questioned next.

"No, I've seen no one except an old organ grinder, and you couldn't class him as a prowler."

"Still, his monkey might have climbed in a window and taken the articles," Nancy suggested.

"I only noticed the organ grinder around two days, and it wasn't on those days that we missed things. Anyway, all of the windows are screened."

"Then that theory won't work," Nancy said, with a troubled frown.

"And it doesn't explain the strange shadows on the walls at night," Rosemary added.

"No. I'm afraid we must look for another explanation."

"I'm more troubled about the shadows than anything else. It's getting to a point where I don't feel safe to sleep in my own bed. I don't know where it will all end. Floretta says she won't stay in the house another week if things go on as they have been, and I can't say that I blame her. If only something could be done before it's too late!"

"Nancy will help you," Abigail Rowen declared confidently.

"You will, won't you?" Rosemary pleaded.

"I don't know whether I can or not," Nancy said doubtfully. "I'm tremendously interested in your story and I'd like to visit The Mansion some time."

"Oh, when can you come?" Rosemary asked eagerly. "The sooner the better."

Nancy Drew glanced thoughtfully at the watch on her wrist.

"I have my roadster outside. If you wish, I could drive you to your home now and stop there before returning to River Heights."

"Oh, if you only will! Floretta will be so grateful! I don't like to give up the house, but things are becoming unbearable. I am sure you can help us."

"I'll do my best to solve the mystery," Nancy smiled as she arose from her chair. "But I'm not in the least confident. I have a suspicion that your ghost isn't going to be very easy to capture."

CHAPTER VI

The Ghost Calls Again

Nancy Drew said good-bye to Abigail Rowen and, after promising to call again soon, left the cottage with Rosemary Turnbull.

"It's nice of you to offer to take me to The Mansion," Rosemary remarked, as she stepped into the blue roadster. "I came by bus you know, and it's a slow, tiresome ride that way. Floretta will be delighted to see me back home earlier than I had planned."

"Is your sister inclined to be nervous?"

"Oh, yes. The slightest thing sets her off. She wouldn't stay at The Mansion alone at night for anything in the world."

"I don't wonder she is nervous. So many strange things have happened there."

"Floretta is certain The Mansion is haunted. I keep telling myself I don't believe in ghosts, and I don't—but those shadows!" Rosemary shuddered. "There's something uncanny about it."

From the general conversation Nancy Drew

had gathered that Rosemary Turnbull was not the type of woman to be easily frightened. She was eager to visit the old stone house, for she felt that she had encountered a genuine mystery.

"Have you told anyone about the strange happenings?" she inquired presently.

Rosemary shook her head.

"Only the sheriff, and he just sniffed. Seemed to think someone was playing a joke on us. To-day I told Abigail Rowen, but otherwise I haven't mentioned it to a soul. You see, I thought that if we should want to sell, the rumor that the house was haunted wouldn't help the sale."

"Hardly," Nancy replied. "But you don't wish to sell, do you?"

"Only as a last resort."

Nancy drove rapidly, for the hour was late and she feared that unless she hurried she would not reach her home before dark. When at last she did reach Cliffwood it was nearly dusk.

Rosemary directed her to The Mansion, which was located in an isolated spot on the outskirts of Cliffwood. Through the tall oak and maple trees which partially hid the house from the road, Nancy Drew caught her first glimpse of the place. She was a little startled, for with its two large turrets at the front, the

Turnbull residence was not unlike a ruined castle.

It was a large, massive structure, built of white stone which, with the passing of the decades, had blackened and crumbled. Undoubtedly, in years gone by it had deserved the title of "mansion," but now it could boast little of its old glory. With the ebb of the Turnbull fortune, the house had fallen into decay.

As Nancy drove up the winding driveway she could not help but notice the ghostlike shadows which the trees, swaying in the breeze, cast on the stone walls. A feeling of uneasiness came over her, a sensation which she was at a loss to explain.

"There's something creepy about the place," she thought. "As Miss Rosemary said, it's a perfect habitat for a ghost."

Nancy was not superstitious and certainly she did not believe in ghosts, but it seemed to her that the very air about the old place was oppressive. Perhaps Rosemary Turnbull had experienced the same sensation, for she turned her eyes toward the second story.

"I don't see a light in Floretta's room," she observed. "I do hope nothing has happened while I have been away."

Nancy stopped the roadster in front of the house and Rosemary alighted.

"You're coming in, aren't you?" she inquired hopefuly.

Nancy hesitated.

"I intended to, but it's growing so late. I promised father I'd be home before dark."

"It's only a short way to River Heights from here. Floretta will be disappointed if you don't come in for a few minutes at least. I want you to hear her version of the mystery."

"I am eager to hear it, too," Nancy declared, switching off the motor. "All right, I'll come in even if it is late. Dad will forgive me his time."

Rosemary fitted her latchkey into the lock and opened the heavy front door.

"We've thought it best to keep the house locked the last few weeks," she explained.

As Nancy Drew stepped inside she noticed that the entire house had the appearance of having been built in more opulent times than the present. The rooms were spacious, especially the living room which was furnished with old-fashioned Colonial furniture. The walls were adorned with massive, gold-framed portraits, obviously of ancestors of the Turnbull line.

As Nancy gazed at the pictures she realized that once the Turnbulls had been the leading family in Cliffwood. They had been a proud family, but with Rosemary and Floretta the line would die out. Little remained of a fortune which had once been large. Rosemary and Floretta, while not poor, had an income only sufficient for their needs. Yet because they were the last of the Turnbulls, they were welcome in the best of society.

"My great great grandfather," Rosemary commented, indicating one of the pictures which had attracted Nancy's interest. "He fought in the Revolution. I am sure if he were living to-day no ghost would dare invade The Mansion," and Rosemary smiled slightly.

Nancy did not reply, for at that moment an elderly lady came hurrying down the stairway to the living room. In appearance she closely resembled Rosemary, though she lacked her sister's firm chin. Nancy knew at once that it was Floretta. She saw, too, that something had disturbed the woman, for she was so agitated that she failed to note the presence of a visitor.

"Oh, Rosemary," she burst out, "why did you leave me here alone? I knew something terrible would happen!"

"Floretta, you—you haven't seen anything?" Rosemary demanded shakily.

"It's my diamond bar pin! It's gone!"

"Oh, Floretta, are you sure? Perhaps you misplaced it."

"No, it's gone. I've looked everywhere. Oh, what shall I do? I can't bear to lose it!" Floretta turned and saw Nancy for the first time. She made a valiant attempt to compose herself. "I beg your pardon," she said somewhat stiffly.

Rosemary introduced Nancy Drew and explained that the young girl had offered to help solve the baffling mystery.

"You've come just in time," Floretta declared. "Oh, if only you can tell me what became of my bar pin! It was an heirloom. We've had it in the family for years."

"When did you have it last?" Nancy asked quietly.

"Only this afternoon. I was dressing in my room and was just completing my toilet when I heard the iceman at the back door. I dropped my bar pin on the dresser and hurried downstairs to let him into the kitchen."

"Were you gone long?" Nancy interrupted.

"Only a few minutes. Not more than ten at the most. When I came back my pin was gone!"

"Are you certain it didn't drop to the floor, or perhaps fall behind the dresser?"

"Oh, I've looked everywhere!" Floretta sank into a chair and buried her head in her hands. "I'm just sick about it. I wouldn't have lost it for anything in the world."

Rosemary went to her sister and tried to comfort her.

"We'll find the pin, Floretta. I'm sure it will turn up somewhere."

She spoke with confidence but nevertheless turned uneasy eyes upon Nancy.

"Perhaps a bird flew in at an open window and took the pin," Nancy suggested.

"Oh, I'm sure that couldn't have happened," Floretta insisted. "But if you'd like to see the room I'll be glad to show it to you."

She led the way up the narrow circular stairs and Nancy and Rosemary followed. Floretta's room was in the east wing.

"Is this the top floor?" Nancy questioned.

"The attic is above," Rosemary responded. She attempted to smile. "There's no ghost up there, though. I know, because I looked myself."

Floretta's room was small. Nancy noticed that it had only one door which opened into the hall. There were two windows, both screened.

"I left the pin right here," Floretta said, indicating the dressing table. "A bird couldn't have taken it."

"I see now," Nancy said quietly.

She crossed the room and examined the screens carefully. Apparently they had not been touched, for an accumulation of dust was undisturbed.

"I know someone entered my room while I was talking with the iceman," Floretta declared firmly. "Oh, I don't want to stay in this horrible house another night!"

"It's apparent no one entered by means of the windows," Nancy said quietly. "Tell me, from where you stood in the kitchen could you see the stairway?"

"Why, I could have if I had looked, I suppose. The kitchen door was open."

"You saw no one go up the stairs?"

"Not a soul. But someone might have entered the house when I had my back turned."

"Weren't the doors locked?"

"Yes, I had forgotten that."

"And if anyone had gone up those stairs wouldn't you have heard them?"

"I think I would have," Floretta admitted. "The stairs are old and they creak."

"Then how did the thief get in?" Rosemary cried. "Floretta's bar pin couldn't have walked off by itself!"

"I wish I could tell you what became of the pin, but I can't," Nancy said regretfully. "I'm as puzzled as you are."

As she spoke she turned and for the first time noticed a closet door. Was it possible that the thief had entered the house early in the day and had hidden in the closet, biding an opportune time to snatch the pin?

Floretta divined Nancy's thought and a look of horror came over her face.

"Oh, you don't suppose someone has been spying upon us?" she demanded fearfully. "I never once thought of that closet! What if there's someone in there now?"

Rosemary laughed nervously.

"Don't be silly, Floretta."

However, she eyed the closet door with misgiving and made no effort to investigate.

"Just to make sure there's no one inside I'll have a look," Nancy remarked.

She crossed the room and paused before the closet door. Hesitating only an instant, she jerked it open.

CHAPTER VII

What Can It Mean?

"Empty!" Nancy Drew announced, as she flung open the closet door and looked carefully inside. "There's no one here now, at least!"

Floretta, who had been clinging to her sister, relaxed her hold, but continued to gaze uneasily about the bedroom as though expecting to find the thief in plain sight.

"I'm afraid it's a case for the police," Nancy said thoughtfully.

"Oh, we don't want to call them," Rosemary protested quickly. "They will only laugh."

"We talked to them once about strange things that have been going on here, and they weren't interested. They seemed to think someone was trying to play a joke on us, and they didn't even send a man to investigate," Floretta added.

"If only you will take the case, Miss Drew," Rosemary begged, "we'll be glad to pay you well for your work."

"But I'm not a detective," Nancy protested

"We heard about the clever way you helped the Horner girls and Abigail Rowen. Surely, you can help us. We need help so desperately."

"I'll be glad to do anything I can," Nancy promised willingly. "But of course I'll not take money."

"But it wouldn't be fair of us to ask you——"

"I am really tremendously interested in the mystery. I'll have a lot of fun trying to solve it. Whether I can do it or not is another matter. There really are no clues with which to start. If I could spend a night or so here——"

"You're more than welcome to come and visit us if you will," Rosemary told her.

"But you come at your own risk," Floretta added.

"I'll talk with father this evening and ask him if I may come," Nancy promised.

"How will you notify us?" Floretta asked. "We have no telephone."

"Oh, I'll send a note. I think it wise not to advertise the real purpose of my visit."

"A good idea," Rosemary agreed. "Floretta and I will take care not to mention it to anyone."

Nancy glanced at her watch.

"I must dash for home now, or father will be worried to death."

Hastily saying good-bye, she left the house and sprang into her roadster. In a few minutes she had reached the main road and was driving swiftly toward River Heights.

"I've certainly struck a real mystery," she mused thoughtfully, as she drove along the smooth road. "The Mansion is haunted all right, but it's haunted by a flesh and blood ghost unless I miss my guess!"

Nancy Drew had no theory which would explain the strange happenings at The Mansion, but, if her father granted permission, she planned to stay several days at the house and investigate everything thoroughly. What the search would reveal she had no idea, but she felt certain she would unearth valuable clues.

"I'll go home and try to piece things together," she told herself. "That's what a regular detective would do!"

It was after dark when Nancy finally reached home. She flashed into the garage with a skill born of long practice, and hurried guiltily toward the house. As she had expected, her father had reached home ahead of her.

"Nancy, I've been worried about you," he began.

"Don't scold," Nancy begged. "I tried not to break my promise, but I couldn't help it this time. Oh, I had the most exciting afternoon!"

"But exciting adventures are hard on poor old Dad," Mr. Drew chided. "When you didn't get back I thought perhaps you had had car trouble on the road. I was about ready to start after you."

"I'm terribly sorry. Honestly, I am."

Nancy looked so genuinely sorry that Carson Drew promptly forgave her.

"Tell me about your adventure," he suggested.

"Oh, I met two of the dearest ladies. They're rather eccentric but, oh, so charming and nice."

"And you call that an adventure!" and Mr. Drew smiled.

"Of course not. I haven't reached the adventure part of it yet. These ladies live in a haunted house. Of course it isn't really haunted, but strange things are going on there, and they want me to find out what's what." Breathlessly, Nancy poured out her words.

"Not so fast," Carson Drew stopped her. "I can't make head or tail of what you are saying. You met two ladies who live in a haunted house which really isn't haunted. That doesn't make sense."

"Oh, you lawyers are so particular about facts," Nancy sighed.

Beginning at the first of the story, she related everything which had happened at the

Turnbull mansion. Her father listened quietly until she had finished.

"I've heard a great deal about the Turnbull sisters," he remarked. "They come from an excellent family. I believe The Mansion has belonged to the Turnbulls ever since it was built."

"It would be a tragedy to Miss Rosemary and Miss Floretta if they had to sell the place now, Dad. I want so badly to help them. They have invited me to visit them, and I'd like to do it. May I?"

"I don't know what to say, Nancy. From what you've told me I am inclined to believe there may be danger in visiting that house."

"I'll be careful, Dad. It won't be any worse for me to sleep in that house than it is for Rosemary and Floretta Turnbull."

"But you're my daughter."

"If you had been assigned to the case you wouldn't hesitate to stay there at night, would you?"

"No," Carson Drew admitted reluctantly, for he saw that Nancy was neatly cornering him.

"And you've often said you wanted me to grow up self-reliant and brave."

Carson Drew threw up his hands in resignation.

"You win, Nancy. Your eloquence would convince a jury."

"When may I go?"

"Well, let me see. This is Monday." Mr. Drew considered the desk calendar. "I'll be leaving for Chicago myself Thursday——"

"You're going to Chicago? I didn't know that."

"Yes, on a business trip. The matter just came up this afternoon. I'll be gone about a week." He looked speculatively at Nancy. "Wouldn't you like to go along?"

"Oh, of course, but if I do I wouldn't get to visit the Turnbull sisters."

"Are you willing to give up the trip for the chance to ferret out this mystery?"

"Oh, yes."

Carson Drew sighed.

"I guess you're a born detective, Nancy. Well, since your heart is set on it I'll give my consent. You may visit the Turnbulls while I am gone."

"A whole week?"

"Yes, if you like."

"Goody! Goody!" Nancy pranced wildly about the room.

Carson Drew laughed.

"I hope you catch the ghost if it will make you happy." Then the smile faded from his lips. "You'll not run into danger?"

"Not if I see it first."

"Seriously, Nancy, you'll be careful, won't you?"

"Of course."

Carson Drew crossed the room and paused in front of his desk. Unlocking a drawer he took out a shiny object and handed it to his daughted.

"Your revolver, Dad!"

"Yes, I want you to take it with you."

"But I sha'n't need it."

"I hope not. But it pays to be prepared. I'll feel better if I know you have it. The Mansion ghost may turn out to be a livelier one than we expect."

Carson Drew spoke half-jestingly, little suspecting that his observation was a true prophecy.

CHAPTER VIII

The Warning

The next two days following her visit to Cliffwood, Nancy Drew went about the house in a preoccupied state. Alternately quiet and talkative, she was never without an air of suppressed excitement.

In an attempt to strike a plausible explanation for the strange happenings at The Mansion, she reviewed every detail of the story related by the Turnbull sisters.

"It's possible the shadows on the wall at night could have been caused by the wind blowing the trees," she told herself. "Still, Rosemary is a practical woman and I'm sure she wouldn't be frightened by a thing like that."

Before she had visited The Mansion with Rosemary, Nancy had been inclined to suspect that someone was playing a practical joke on the Turnbull sisters, but the loss of the diamond bar pin made such a theory seem unlikely. Without doubt, someone had stolen the pin, but in what manner, she was unable to guess. Apparently, it had vanished into thin air.

The longer Nancy reflected on the mystery the more certain she was that a sinister hand was behind everything. However, she refrained from disclosing this thought to her father lest he reconsider his promise and refuse her permission to visit the old house during the week he was to spend in Chicago.

Carson Drew planned to leave on Thursday. Nancy had written a note to the Turnbull sisters telling them to expect her on Saturday morning. She had taken care not to mention the approaching visit to anyone save her father, and even Hannah Gruen was in ignorance concerning her plans.

On the day set for Mr. Drew's departure, Nancy helped him pack his bag, and then shortly before train time took him to the railroad station in her roadster.

"When shall I expect you home?" Nancy inquired, as they stood on the platform waiting for the train.

"A week from to-day. If you would like me to, I'll stop at Cliffwood on my return trip. Your story has aroused my interest, Nancy. I'm curious to have a look at that old stone mansion."

"Oh, I wish you would stop for me," Nancy declared enthusiastically. She glanced carefully about to see that no one was within hearing distance. "If I haven't solved the mystery by that time you'll help me, won't you?"

"Of course I'll do anything I can, but from what you've told me it sounds like a tough case. I'm not sure that I'll be able to solve it myself. However, if you fail, I'll try it."

The conversation was cut short as a shrill whistle announced the approach of the train.

"I'll telegraph you the exact hour of my arrival in Cliffwood," he said hastily.

"The Turnbulls live some distance from the railroad station, so I'll meet you in the car," Nancy promised.

"And remember—don't run into danger."

The heavy passenger train came pounding and clanging into the station, and Mr. Drew picked up his bag. Kissing Nancy good-bye, he made a dash for the Pullman cars, which were at the rear of the train, far down the track.

Nancy waited until the train pulled out and then slowly made her way back to the automobile. Now that her father had actually departed, she felt lonesome.

"I may as well stop at Helen Corning's before I go home," she decided as she stepped into the roadster. Helen Corning had been her chum for years.

Accordingly, she called at the home of her

chum and was pleased to find her there. Helen promptly tempted her into a lively game of tennis, and before Nancy realized it, the afternoon was nearly gone.

"You must stay for dinner," Helen urged. "It won't be any fun eating at home all alone."

"But Hannah is expecting me."

"We can telephone her."

"Oh, all right," Nancy gave in.

Not only did she stay for dinner, but she remained during the evening, for Helen would not permit her to go.

"Remember the fun we had at Moon Lake last summer?" Helen asked her. "You know, I never did entirely forgive you for cheating me out of a share in your adventure. Why didn't you tell me you were going to chase robbers that day when you left camp?"

"I didn't know it myself then."

"Well, if you ever stumble upon another mystery, I want you to take me in on it!"

Nancy was on the verge of telling Helen about her proposed trip to The Mansion, but she could not bring herself to the point of revealing the secret. Helen's intentions were of the best, but she was a natural born gossip and Nancy doubted that it would be possible for her to keep the matter to herself.

"It might do a great deal of harm if it were rumored why I am leaving town," she thought. "No, I'll tell Helen after I return."

It was late when Nancy reached home and the housekeeper had retired.

"I'm too sleepy to pack my bag to-night," she decided as she locked the doors and windows. "I'll do it the first thing in the morning."

But in the morning there were other matters which claimed Nancy's attention. She had promised the housekeeper a week's vacation during her visit in Cliffwood, and before the house could be closed there were many things to be done. The entire day had slipped away almost before she realized it.

"Miss Nancy, if you don't mind, I'll go to a moving picture show with my sister," the housekeeper said to her after the dinner dishes had been cleared away.

"Why, of course, Hannah," she agreed generously. "I don't mind in the least. I'll be busy with my packing."

As soon as Hannah had left the house, Nancy went directly to her room and began sorting out the dresses that she planned to take with her to The Mansion. It was ten minutes after eleven when she finished.

"There, I guess that's all," she decided.

"Oh, no, I've forgotten the revolver Dad gave me. I must take that!"

She hurried downstairs and went directly to the desk where the revolver had been left. But with her hand on the drawer, Nancy hesitated.

Uneasily, she glanced about the room. For a reason she could not explain, she felt that someone was watching her.

"I guess my nerves are getting jumpy," she thought. "I do wish Hannah would come home."

Upon impulse, she moved toward the window. As she took a step forward, she thought she heard a step on the porch. Was it only imagination or was someone really prowling about the house?

Before she could make a move to investigate, the doorbell rang sharply.

Nancy started.

"It must be Hannah," she assured herself. "Probably she forgot her key."

But as she crossed the room she distinctly heard the steps creak under the weight of some person. Hesitating but an instant, she opened the door.

There was no one in sight. Wonderingly, Nancy stepped out upon the veranda and glanced up and down the street.

"That's strange," she murmured uncomfortably.

She went to the edge of the porch and peered in the direction of the hedge. Was it possible someone was hiding in the bushes? A careful survey disclosed no human form.

As she turned to go inside the house, her eyes fell upon a white envelope near the door. Curiously, Nancy picked it up and held it to the light.

"Why, it's addressed to me!" she gasped in astonishment, as she made out the bold scrawl.

Hastily entering the house and closing the door behind her, Nancy Drew ripped open the envelope. As she scanned the note, the color faded from her face.

"An anonymous message!" she whispered. "Someone has sent me a threatening letter!"

CHAPTER IX

The Anonymous Message

Nancy Drew sank down upon the davenport and studied the note which had just been delivered at her door. The message was brief, but its words carried an import of veiled violence which mystified and frightened her. It read:

"Be warned in time. Keep away from the Turnbull house."

The threatening communication was unsigned but was written in a bold scrawl, and, Nancy fancied, was unmistakably the handwriting of a man.

"Who could have sent it?" she asked herself, in amazement. "Why, I've taken special pains not to let anyone know I am going to the Turnbull house. Even Hannah doesn't know I am to visit there."

How could anyone have learned of her plans? Nancy Drew turned this question over in her mind as she sat propped up with pillows in a corner of the big davenport, the very picture of a pretty girl in a brown study over some knotty problem. The more she thought about it, the knottier her problem became, for she had communicated with Rosemary and Floretta by writing, and unless her note to them had been intercepted in the mail, there was no way, to her knowledge, that the information could have become known to a third person.

"I'm almost tempted to believe in ghosts myself," she thought. "It's positively uncanny!" She reflected a moment and then chuckled: "But, anyway, I don't believe the ghost is a very brave one, or he wouldn't be afraid to have me on his trail."

As she considered the possibility of danger connected with her visit to the old mansion, the smile faded from her face and all facetious thoughts about ghosts passed from her mind. The note had frightened her, but it had not deterred her in her purpose to do all within her power to solve the mystery surrounding The Mansion. Nancy possessed the fighting instincts of her father, and it would take more than a threat to keep her away from the Turnbull house. She was convinced that underhand work was going on at The Mansion and she was determined to expose it if it were possible to do so.

"I think Dad was wise to suggest that I take

his revolver," she told herself. "And I'll take plenty of ammunition, too! Enough to annihilate an army! Though, truth to tell, I don't know whether I could hit the broad side of a barn or not."

Getting up from the davenport, Nancy crossed over to the desk, and with a glance at the window shades to see that they were down, removed the revolver from the drawer. Taking it upstairs, she placed it carefully in her traveling bag. As she started back down the stairs, she heard a light step on the porch.

She paused and listened.

"I wonder if I'm to get another note?" flashed through her mind.

Before she could move forward, the door opened and Hannah Gruen came in.

"Oh, it's you," Nancy murmured in relief.

"Why, yes. Who did you think it was?"

"Well, I didn't know," and Nancy smiled. "I wouldn't have been much surprised if a ghost had walked in."

"A ghost?" Hannah asked in alarm. "What do you mean?"

"Oh, nothing," Nancy assured her hastily. "I was only joking."

Before the housekeeper could question her further, the girl said good night and retreated to her bedroom.

"I'll not let that anonymous note disturb my

sleep," she told herself resolutely, as she tumbled into bed, "and to-morrow I'll start for The Mansion just as I planned."

After she had finished her breakfast the next morning, Nancy Drew took leave of the housekeeper, and, closing up the house, started off for Cliffwood in her roadster.

There was not a sign of life about the old stone house as she drove up, and she began to wonder if anything had happened to Rosemary and Floretta since her last visit.

However, before she could lift the knocker on the front door, Rosemary greeted her.

"I saw you coming up the drive. Oh, you don't know how glad we are that you have come!" she declared cordially. "You see, we were afraid you might change your mind. We couldn't have blamed you if you had."

"I hope nothing has happened since I was here the other day," Nancy said quickly.

"Oh, it's been almost unbearable. We had made up our minds to leave the place if you didn't come to-day."

Rosemary's face was strained, and Nancy thought she looked as though she had not slept for several nights. The ordeal of remaining in the house was gradually wearing her down.

"Last night we heard music again," she said, in a very low tone.

"What sort of music?"

"It seemed to come from a stringed instrument. It might have been a guitar."

"From what part of the house?"

"That was the strange part of it. The sound wasn't localized. It seemed to move from one part of the house to another."

"Did you hear the music distinctly?"

"No; the sound was muffled, as though it were a long way off. Oh, it was almost ghostly!" Rosemary shuddered and turned appealing eyes upon Nancy. "Tell me, do you believe in the supernatural?"

"I am almost certain your house is not haunted," Nancy returned firmly, for she saw that Rosemary's iron nerve was beginning to go back on her. "How long did the music last?"

"About half an hour, I should judge."

"Did Miss Floretta hear it, too?"

"Oh, yes. She's positively ill this morning. She didn't get out of bed. We'll go to her room now if you like."

"Perhaps it would be better not to disturb her."

"Oh, she wanted to see you just as soon as you arrived."

Rosemary led the way through the long, dark corridor and to the stairway.

"I'll show you to your room first and then

you can talk with Floretta," she told Nancy when they reached the upper hall.

Rosemary opened a door and permitted Nancy to enter ahead of her. The bedroom was a large, comfortable one with an old-fashioned canopy bed and heavy mahogany furniture.

"I have assigned you the room right next my own," Rosemary explained. "If anything should happen during the night you could rap on the wall or cry out and I would hear you."

Nancy nodded soberly.

"And the key is in the door," Rosemary continued. "Floretta and I always lock our doors."

"I will lock mine too," Nancy promised.

"Are you certain you want to go through with it?" Rosemary questioned anxiously. "If anything should happen to you I'd never forgive myself."

"I don't believe anything serious will happen."

"I wish I could feel as confident," Rosemary sighed. "Shall we go to Floretta now?"

"Yes, I am ready. I will unpack my bag later."

Nancy followed Rosemary down the hall and they entered the bedroom in the east wing.

"Welcome to the haunted house," Floretta murmured as a greeting to the girl. She was propped up in bed with cushions and her face was white and haggard. A tray on a table near the bed had been left practically untouched.

"Floretta, you didn't eat your breakfast," Rosemary chided gently.

"Oh, I couldn't, Rosemary. I'm so upset. I can't stay in this horrible place much longer."

"Miss Drew is here to help us," Rosemary responded quietly.

"But can she? I'm beginning to doubt that anyone can help us!"

"Nonsense! You mustn't let your nerves get the best of you!"

"I think I can help you." Nancy smiled reassuringly. "At least I will do my best. I intend to go all over the house and see if I can locate secret panels or trapdoors."

"I don't believe it will do any good," Floretta declared pessimistically. "I never heard of anything like that in the house."

"I may as well have a look, anyway," Nancy said easily. She remembered something which she intended to ask the Turnbull sisters. "Tell me, did you mention to anyone that I was coming here for a visit?"

"No," Rosemary answered promptly. "We took care not to mention it to a soul."

"Of course we talked about your note when it came," Floretta added. "But we didn't let out a hint of its contents to anyone. Why do you ask?"

Nancy hesitated, then deciding that it could do no particular harm to tell the Turnbull sisters of the note she had received, she related what had happened the previous night.

"Someone warned you not to come here?" Floretta gasped. "Why, how could the news have gotten out?"

"I wish I knew," Nancy admitted. "It would seem as though the walls have ears!" She lowered her voice. "Even now, someone may be listening to every word we say!"

CHAPTER X

An Unfruitful Search

Nancy Drew's presence in The Mansion had a wholesome effect upon the Turnbull sisters, for soon after her arrival they became more cheerful. Floretta announced that she felt a great deal better and insisted upon getting up and dressing. To the surprise of her sister she appeared most cheerful when she came downstairs for luncheon.

"Tell me, does this house have any particular history?" Nancy questioned, as the three sat at the table.

"Oh, yes, indeed," Rosemary responded proudly. "It was built in the early days when stone houses were out of the ordinary. Of course The Mansion has been remodeled many times, but the original walls still stand. The property has never passed from the Turnbull family."

"To your knowledge there are no secret panels or trapdoors in the house?"

"I know of none. However, Floretta and I

never were interested in such things until recently, and I'll admit we haven't gone over the house carefully. It's possible something like that was built-in when the house was remodeled in Civil War times. As a protective measure, you know."

"Then, if you have no objection, I believe I'll have a look around and see if I can locate anything unusual."

"Certainly," Rosemary assured her. "You're free to do anything you like, and we'll help you all we can. Where will you start?"

"I may as well begin in the attic and work down."

"If you go up there you'll need candles. It's very dark. You see, we've never had the house wired for electricity."

Rosemary hurried to the kitchen, and returned in a few minutes with half a dozen large tallow candles. Before concentrating her attention upon the attic, Nancy made a preliminary survey of the entire mansion.

The house consisted of fifteen large rooms. On the first floor, in addition to the kitchen, butler's pantry, and dining room, there was a drawing room, a library, a sun parlor and a reception hall. Directly beneath the first floor was the basement, which had been broken up into storerooms.

The second floor was devoted to bedchambers. Rosemary explained that one wing of the house had been shut off for years, and this portion of the house at once aroused Nancy's interest. However, a casual survey of the rooms reveal nothing which would indicate that anyone had visited them in the last six years. A thick accumulation of dust was undisturbed.

"We'll try the attic first," Nancy decided. "Later, I'll go over these other rooms more carefully."

Single file, Nancy and the two ladies trudged up the narrow stairs leading to the attic. As Nancy opened a door at the head of the stairs, a gust of wind struck her candle and extinguished the flame. Quickly lighting it, she stepped into the attic.

She glanced about curiously, flashing the light into every nook and corner. The attic appeared little different from others Nancy had visited. It was filled with pieces of discarded furniture. A tall highboy stood in one corner, a broken rocking chair in another, and boxes were piled everywhere.

Systematicaly, Nancy poked into the boxes and went over the walls inch by inch. The latter had a hollow sound, but she was unable to find a spring which would open a panel. If the walls guarded a secret, they guarded it well.

"I guess there's nothing here," Nancy admitted after she had spent nearly an hour in the attic.

She was reluctant to leave, for although she had unearthed nothing, she could not help but feel that she had overlooked something of vital importance.

"I was afraid you wouldn't find anything," Rosemary commented, as she turned toward the stairs. "Now where?"

"Shall we try the basement?"

The three made their way cautiously down the stairs to the first floor and from there to the kitchen. As they descended into the dark cellar, an unpleasant musty odor assailed their nostrils.

A few minutes search convinced Nancy that the basement was not worth bothering about. The floors and walls had been covered with cement and offered no possibility of a trapdoor. However, before returning to the first floor, she looked carefully about in the storerooms to make certain that no one was hiding there.

"Well, our search wasn't very well rewarded," Nancy admitted, after the three had returned to the kitchen. "But I'm not ready to give up yet. I intend to have another look to-morrow."

The investigation of the attic and the basement had taken the better part of the afternoon, and already shadows were beginning to lurk in the nooks and crannies. With the approach of night the house seemed to take on a more formidable atmosphere.

Dinner at The Mansion was rather a strained, formal affair. Rosemary and Nancy made an attempt to keep up a conversation, but without much success. There was a tenseness in the air which everyone felt.

After dinner the three adjourned to the drawing room. Rosemary sat down at the piano and tried to play, but Nancy noticed that her hands trembled. After a time, she gave it up.

Floretta was even less composed than her sister. She sat rigidly on the sofa, with hands tightly clasped. Involuntarily, her eyes roved about the room as though she were looking for someone.

"What an odd piece of furniture," Nancy commented in an attempt to start a conversation.

"Which piece do you mean?" Rosemary questioned.

"The sofa. I never saw one like it."

"I don't wonder. It's built in."

"Built in? How odd. I've seen built-in bookcases and window seats, but I never heard of a built-in sofa."

"It was our great grandfather's idea," Floretta explained. "I never could see any sense in it myself. I'd much rather have a sofa that could be moved about."

At nine o'clock, Nancy announced that she would retire, and in obvious relief Floretta and Rosemary arose to follow her example.

"Don't forget to lock your door," Rosemary warned her guest, as she said good night at the head of the stairs. "And if anything should happen—scream. We'll hear you."

As soon as she was alone in her bedchamber, Nancy Drew locked the door. Then she made a hasty examination of the closet. There was nothing inside. She looked under the bed.

"There's nothing like caution," she assured herself. "I don't believe a ghost will get in here very easily, but just the same I'll be prepared."

Unlocking her traveling bag she removed the revolver her father had given her and a flashlight she had thoughtfully included as part of her emergency equipment. Carefully loading the revolver, she placed it under her pillow.

"There!" she exclaimed, with satisfaction. "Any ghost that comes prowling about is apt to meet with a warm reception!"

With that, she sprang into bed. She did not intend to fall asleep at once, but before she knew it, she had dozed off. When she awoke the sun was streaming in the bedroom window.

With a start, Nancy Drew opened her eyes

and glanced about the room. So far as she could tell everything was exactly as she had left it. Hurriedly dressing, she went downstairs. Rosemary and Floretta were there ahead of her, and breakfast was nearly ready.

"Did you sleep well?" Rosemary asked her.

"Like a log."

"I scarcely shut my eyes all night."

"But surely nothing happened to alarm you?" she asked.

"No, I didn't hear a sound."

After breakfast Nancy once more began the task of investigating the walls of the various rooms in the hope of discovering a sliding panel. She spent the morning going over the downstairs rooms. She tapped the walls with a small hammer and even looked behind the heavy pictures.

"I'm certain there must be a secret opening in this house somewhere," she told herself. "But it doesn't look as though I am going to find it very easily."

In the afternoon she devoted her attention to the bedrooms, but without success. That night she again slept with the revolver under her pillow.

The next day was a repetition of the one that had gone before. Nancy began to wonder if there really was a mystery connected with the old house.

"Can it be that Rosemary and Floretta only imagine strange things that have been happening?" she asked herself.

That night when she retired, she was half inclined not to place the revolver under her pillow as usual, for it seemed a rather unnecessary precaution. Upon second thought, however, she decided it would be wise not to take a chance.

After climbing into bed and blowing out the light, she did not fall asleep at once. The window curtains were up, permitting the moonlight to stream in, and for some time Nancy watched the shadows of the trees dance on the white walls of the room.

"I wonder if those shadows were the ones Rosemary and Floretta saw?" she thought.

After about half an hour she dozed off, but she did not sleep soundly. She awoke in the middle of the night and found that she could not go back to slumber.

"What is the matter with me?" she asked herself. "I feel just as if something were about to happen!"

The house was as quiet as a tomb. Yet there was something about the silence which was ominous.

"This will never do," Nancy chided herself severely, as she felt a cold chill creeping over her.

Resolutely, she closed her eyes, but sleep would not come. She tried the time-worn device of counting the sheep, but in vain. It was as though a faculty over which she had no control had elected to maintain a vigil. Restlessly, Nancy Drew tossed about.

Then, just as she was sinking into a light sleep, she was aroused rudely. What was it that had awakened her? She sat up in bed and tried to pierce the darkness.

Then she heard a noise which seemed to come from the floor below. There was a dull thud and then a blood-curdling yell! After that—silence.

CHAPTER XI

A Cry in the Night

When the loud, piercing cry echoed through the old stone house, Nancy Drew instinctively clutched the bedclothing about her neck as though by so doing she could protect herself from an unseen danger. An instant she waited, but the cry was not repeated. There was not a sound to be heard anywhere in the house.

Then, with determination, Nancy sprang from the bed and slipped quickly into her dressing gown and put on her bedroom slippers. Reaching under her pillow, she was relieved to find the revolver and flashlight where she had left them.

The stars were no longer shining and the room was so dark that she could not see a foot ahead of her. Switching on the flashlight, she made her way to the door and gave it a pull. It did not open.

"Am I locked in?" Nancy thought in horror.

In her haste and excitement, she had forgotten that she had fastened the door herself. As she remembered, she turned the key in the lock and jerked open the door.

Stepping out into the corridor, she flashed her light about in all directions. There was no one in sight.

Then the door at the end of the hall opened and Floretta half-stumbled, half-fell into the corridor. As she saw the flashlight, she let out a low cry of fright.

"Be quiet!" Nancy warned.

"Oh, I thought it was the ghost!" Floretta chattered. "Did you hear that terrible scream?"

"Yes, I heard it. Where is Miss Rosemary? See if she is all right."

"Oh, if Rosemary has been murdered——"

She broke off as Rosemary came out of her room. She, too, was badly frightened, but she was able to maintain a certain amount of composure. The two sisters huddled together near Nancy. Although nearly thirty years older than the girl, they seemed to look to her for protection.

"The cry came from the floor below, or at least that's the way it sounded to me," Nancy whispered. "We must go down there and find out what has happened."

"Go down there?" Floretta wailed. "Never!"

"Sh!" Nancy warned. "Not so loud. We don't know what danger we are facing."

"We'll be murdered if we go down there,"

Floretta maintained in a slightly lower tone.

"I have a revolver."

"I can't go."

"Then you stay here," Rosemary said brusquely, to hide the tremble in her own voice. "If you're going downstairs, I'll go with you, Nancy."

"And leave me here all alone?" Floretta asked desperately.

"Then come along," Rosemary told her curtly.

Flashlight in hand, Nancy Drew had already started to move toward the steps. Rosemary followed, and Floretta, not to be left alone, brought up the rear.

On the stairway, the three huddled together while Nancy flashed her light about the hall below them. Everything was in perfect order and there was no sign of an intruder.

"It was a ghost! I know it was!" Floretta whispered.

"Be quiet!" Rosemary warned.

Nancy led the way on down the circular stairs. At every step the old boards creaked alarmingly underfoot.

"We're certainly heralding our approach all right," Nancy thought grimly. "I hope someone doesn't take a shot at us!"

This fear she did not communicate to the Turnbull sisters, for she knew that it would take but little to throw them into a frenzy of fright.

Reaching the drawing room, she fumbled about and finally located an oil lamp which she lighted. A survey of the room revealed nothing amiss. Everything seemed in its place, and the trio moved on toward the sun parlor.

"The silver!" Floretta exclaimed suddenly. "Do you suppose it is missing?"

The same thought had just occurred to Nancy, and, turning quickly, she hurried toward the dining room. Floretta and Rosemary followed at a more cautious pace.

The buffet where the silver was kept was locked. Rosemary removed the key from a near-by vase and, fitting it into the lock, opened the door.

"Nothing is missing," she declared, after she had finished counting the silver.

"I don't believe the cry came from this room, anyway," Nancy said thoughtfully. "It seemed to me that it was directly under my bedroom."

"Then the cry must have come from the library," Rosemary announced.

"I thought it seemed to come from that direction, too," Floretta murmured. "It was the most blood-curdling yell I ever heard. Like someone in distress."

"Shall we search the library?" Nancy interrupted.

"Lead the way," Rosemary told her grimly.

With revolver held ready for instant use, Nancy Drew started in the direction of the library. The Turnbull sisters, who still huddled together, kept close behind her. Scarcely had they taken a dozen steps when Floretta paused and looked anxiously back over her shoulder.

"What was that?" she whispered fearfully.

"What?" Nancy asked impatiently, turning around. "I didn't hear anything."

"I thought I heard footsteps behind me," Floretta murmured nervously.

"You must have been mistaken," Rosemary said firmly. "I heard nothing."

Nancy was certain that Floretta's nerves were getting the best of her, but nevertheless, to make sure that they were not being followed, she paused and strained her ears to catch a sound. She could hear nothing.

"You must have been mistaken," she said quietly, again moving on.

In the face of danger, Nancy Drew was cool and collected, but even for her it was a nerve-wracking experience to move through the dimly lighted old mansion, uncertain as to what lay just ahead. At any moment they might be walking into a trap.

She opened the library door cautiously, half-expecting something to spring out and pounce upon her. As she flashed her light about the room she was relieved to see that everything was in order. But was it?

Her eye rested upon a ladder-back chair which had been pushed up against the bookcase. Surely, Rosemary and Floretta would not have left it that way, for they were both excellent housekeepers and meticulous about details.

Rosemary's eyes had fallen upon the same chair.

"Someone has been in here!" she exclaimed.

Her eyes slowly traveled upward to the top of the bookcase. She gave a little scream.

"My silver urn! It's gone! Someone has stolen my urn!"

CHAPTER XII

The Theft

"The silver urn is gone!" Rosemary repeated, as though unable to believe her eyes. "Someone has taken it! And it can never be replaced."

"It was a family heirloom," Floretta added morosely. "We've had it ever since grandmother died. It was handed down from one generation to another."

"It was valuable, too," Rosemary went on. "It was solid silver. We had been offered five hundred dollars for it by a jeweler, but of course we refused the offer. Oh, I can't bear to lose it!" She sank into a chair and looked as though she were about to cry.

"Perhaps we'll find it somewhere," Nancy offered hopefully. "Are you certain it was left in the library?"

"Oh, yes, it was on the top of the bookcase. We've kept it there for years."

"First a spoon, then a pocketbook, next my pin, and now the urn," Floretta reviewed pessimistically. "It's too much. I know there's a ghost in this house."

"A ghost wouldn't have needed a chair to reach the top of the bookcase," Nancy commented dryly.

"That's so," Rosemary agreed. "The chair is pushed up against the bookcase! But how did the thief get into the house?"

"If we knew the answer to that question, I think the mystery would be solved," Nancy returned. "Were the doors all locked last night before you went to bed?"

"Oh, yes, I was very careful."

"And the windows?"

"All bolted."

"I can't understand it," Nancy murmured, perplexed.

She examined the room as carefully as she could in the dim light but was unable to find any additional traces of the midnight prowler.

"The thief seems to have vanished into thin air," she said at last. "I don't believe there is any use to search to-night. We may as well go back to bed."

"I couldn't sleep a wink," Floretta interposed. "I am going to sit up the rest of the night."

"So am I," Rosemary added.

"Then we may as well bring our blankets down here," Nancy declared. "I don't think the thief will return to-night, but at least we can be prepared."

Accordingly, the three settled themselves in comfortable chairs, and spent the remainder of the night snugly wrapped in warm blankets. Nancy and Rosemary occasionally dozed off into a light slumber, but Floretta was too nervous to permit herself to go to sleep. Although the light was burning, her eyes continually roved about the room, fearfully searching the darker corners.

At the first indication of dawn, Rosemary, with Nancy assisting her, prepared breakfast. Hot coffee went a long way toward reviving the spirits of the trio. And with the rising of the sun, the old house seemed less oppressive and fearful.

As soon as breakfast was over, Nancy set herself to the task of going over the library minutely. She examined the walls inch by inch, but found no indication of a secret panel. With Rosemary's help, she even moved the heavy bookcase, but there was nothing behind it. The furniture occupied but little of her time, for with the exception of a built-in sofa similar to the one in the drawing room, it was all very ordinary and offered no possibility of a hiding place. Nancy did examine the bookcase and the chairs for fingerprints, but her search was not rewarded. There was not a single clue which pointed to the identity of the thief.

Nor was the missing urn found anywhere in the place. All day Nancy searched, but in vain. She was bitterly disappointed, for she had hoped to be able to help Rosemary and Floretta. The ordeal of the night had frightened them a great deal, and they began to talk seriously of leaving the house at the end of the week.

"It will be better to close it up than to endure another week like the past one," Rosemary admitted. "I don't like to be driven away, but I see no other way."

Nancy said nothing, but mentally resolved that she would never leave The Mansion until she had solved the mystery. When her father arrived on his way home from Chicago, she would tell him everything and turn the case over to him.

The next two days and nights were uneventful, greatly to the surprise of everyone. Rosemary and Floretta began to show the effects of the strain under which they labored.

"I declare, I'd almost as soon something would happen as to keep thinking it's going to every minute," Rosemary sighed.

With the passing of the days, Nancy Drew became quiet and thoughtful. She had a new worry which she did not communicate to the Turnbull sisters.

When her father had left for Chicago he had promised that he would return within a week and that he would send her a telegram stating the exact hour he expected to arrive in Cliffwood. For several days Nancy had been anxiously looking for the message, but it had not arrived. Why had her father failed to keep his promise?

"It's possible Dad didn't get his business accomplished as quickly as he expected," she assured herself. "I'll probably get the telegram to-morrow."

But the expected message did not arrive on the following day, and now Nancy began to worry in earnest. Surely, her father would have wired her if he had been delayed, she told herself. What could have happened?

"Perhaps he decided not to stop at Cliffwood, and went on to River Heights," she reasoned.

Glancing at the calendar she saw that it was a full week since her father had left home. By this time she had expected to return to River Heights herself, and she had asked Hannah to open the house before her arrival.

"If only there were a telephone here," she fretted. "I could call home and find out if Dad is there yet."

The more she thought of it, the more anxious she became, and at last, to relieve her mind, she decided to drive to Cliffwood and make the telephone call. This intention she communicated to Rosemary and Floretta.

"You'll not be gone long, will you?" Rosemary questioned anxiously. "We've decided not to stay in this house another night alone. When you leave, we're going too."

"I'll be back in a few minutes," Nancy promised. "I only want to make a telephone call."

"I'm sorry we haven't one here," Rosemary apologized. "It's so much bother to go into Cliffwood."

"I really don't mind at all. I'll enjoy the ride."

As Nancy left The Mansion behind, she breathed more freely. There was something about the place that was oppressive. She drove rapidly and soon reached the main part of Cliffwood. Entering a corner drug store, she telephoned to her own home. After a short wait, Hannah Gruen answered.

"Is my father home yet?" Nancy asked, after a few preliminary remarks.

"No, I haven't heard from him since he left," came the response.

Nancy hung up the receiver and leaned against the side of the telephone booth. What could it mean? Why had her father failed to notify anyone of his change of plans? It was not at all like him.

"I have a notion to telegraph to Chicago and find out if he has left there," she thought. "I believe I have the address of the firm he went to see."

Opening her purse, she fished about and after pulling out several wrong cards, found the one for which she was searching.

"Now to find a telegraph office," she decided, as she left the drug store.

She found one only a few doors away, and, having entered, wrote out a brief message and handed it to the clerk at the desk.

"When the answer comes have it sent to the Turnbull Mansion," she told the man.

After paying the charges, she left the office and slowly made her way back to the roadster.

"Now, back to the haunted house," she told herself grimly. "I'm beginning to feel that I'll never solve the mystery by myself. I'll be glad when Dad gets here so he can help me."

As she approached The Mansion, Nancy's attention was attracted to another stone house only a short distance away. In general appearance it bore a striking resemblance to The Mansion.

"I wonder who lives there?" she thought. "I must inquire when I get back to The Mansion."

However, for the time being, Nancy was too troubled about her father to devote much thought to the mystery of the old house, and before she reached The Mansion she had forgotten the question she had intended to ask.

The evenings at The Mansion were all alike. Dinner was served at seven o'clock in the big, gloomy dining room, and after that the three adjourned to the drawing room. There was no radio and no evening paper. With the deepening of the shadows, the conversation became stilted and difficult. By nine o'clock everyone was glad of the opportunity to retire.

All afternoon Nancy had waited hopefully for an answer to her telegram, but it had not arrived. She would have made another trip to the telegraph office in the evening, but she knew that Rosemary and Floretta would be afraid to stay in the house alone.

At nine o'clock Nancy went to her room, but she did not fall asleep for hours.

"I have the strangest feeling," she thought. "It's just as though something had happened to Dad. Of course it's silly of me!"

But try as she would, she could not free herself of the conviction, and when she arose in the morning it was still with her. She ate very little for breakfast, but her lack of appetite passed unnoticed by the Turnbull sisters. As she was about to leave the table, there came a ring of the front doorbell.

Rosemary and Floretta exchanged frightened glances.

"Who—who can it be, do you suppose?" Floretta stammered.

"I'll go," Nancy said quickly. "I think it must be for me."

She left the dining room and hastened to open the front door. As she had expected, it was a uniformed messenger boy.

"Telegram for Nancy Drew," he said curtly.

"I am Miss Drew."

"Then sign here."

Nancy complied with the request and eagerly accepted the yellow envelope. As she tore open the flap and scanned the message a frightened look came over her face. The telegram had been sent by the law firm in Chicago and confirmed her worst fears.

The message read:

"Carson Drew left here two days ago."

CHAPTER XIII

Another Surprise

For a full minute Nancy Drew stood staring blankly at the telegram in her hand. She read it a second time, although she knew every word by memory.

Worry assailed her anew. If her father had left Chicago two days before, as the telegram indicated, he would have reached Cliffwood before this even if he had come on the slowest train. Surely, something must have happened to him en route. What had delayed him?

After a moment's reflection, Nancy entered the house, intending to tell the Turnbull sisters about the telegram and ask their advice. She was destined never to carry the thought into action, for as she closed the door behind her she heard a wild shriek from above. It seemed to come from Floretta's room.

Fearing the worst, Nancy sprang toward the stairs and took them two at a time. Rosemary came running from the kitchen.

Reaching Floretta's room, Nancy thrust open the door.

"What is it?" she cried.

Floretta stood in the center of the room, wringing her hands in anguish.

"My dresses have been stolen!"

"Your dresses?" Nancy echoed.

"Yes, while we were at breakfast. Someone entered my room and took three of my best black silk dresses. And that isn't the worst. Look up there!"

Wonderingly, Nancy turned her eyes toward a picture which hung over the bed. What she saw caused her to gasp in astonishment.

On the frame perched two live canary birds!

"Oh!" Rosemary screamed. She had entered the room behind Nancy and her eyes had fallen upon the picture frame.

"It's wizardry!" Floretta moaned.

Cautiously, Nancy moved toward the picture.

"Don't touch those birds," Rosemary advised.

"Why, they're only tame little canaries," Nancy said, gently removing one from the frame. "See!"

"Don't bring that bird near me!" Floretta cried. "It's an evil omen."

"I never heard of a canary being called an omen of bad luck," Nancy returned, studying the bird curiously. "A canary is a rather happy little bird. This one is, anyway."

"Get them out of the house," Floretta pleaded.

Obligingly, Nancy opened the window and set the two canaries free.

"How did they ever get in here, anyway?" Rosemary demanded. "We never had a bird in our lives."

Nancy was dumbfounded. Never had she heard of a more puzzling mystery. Had the canaries been left in the room by the same person who had stolen Floretta's dresses? Unquestionably, the birds could not have flown in a window, for they were kept carefully screened.

So many strange things had occurred in the house. Unexplainable music and shadows, and the sound of footsteps in the night. Then a spoon had disappeared, next a pocketbook, a diamond pin, an urn, and now Floretta's silk dresses.

Nancy lost no time in examining the closet and the walls of the room, but she could find no clue which suggested in what manner an entrance had been effected. Apparently, the windows had not been opened.

Nancy felt almost humiliated. She had promised to help Floretta and Rosemary, and so far she had not even gained a clue! Many things had happened under her very nose, and yet she had been unable to put her hands on the thief. There must be an explanation for everything if only she could think of it!

As she stood absorbed in her own unpleasant thoughts, a sudden idea came to her.

"Do you know of anyone who wants to force you out of this house?" she demanded.

Rosemary shook her head.

"Why, no. Why should anyone want to do that?"

"Is there anyone who wants to buy the house?"

"We've had several offers from real estate men. There's some talk that the city wants this house for a historical museum."

"And the real estate men are trying to get it cheap in the hope of selling to the city and making a neat profit for themselves," Nancy summarized shrewdly.

"That's about it."

"You don't intend to sell?"

"We didn't—until lately. At least not unless we could get our price for it. Now, we'd be lucky to sell it for anything, I guess. No one wants a haunted house."

Nancy was eager to learn more, for now she felt that she had stumbled upon her first clue. She was convinced that someone was trying to force the Misses Turnbull from their home and, by frightening them, induce them to sell The Mansion at a low figure.

"Who has tried to purchase the place?" she asked quickly.

"Well, there's John O'Conley," Floretta told her.

"What sort of man is he?"

"Oh, I'm sure he is honest. We've known him all our lives."

"And there was H. D. Fellows, another real estate agent," Rosemary added thoughtfully. "He made us a very straightforward offer, but he wasn't willing to meet our price. However, he was very nice about it when we told him we wouldn't sell."

"Were there any others?"

"Oh, Nathan Gombet! But we didn't consider his offer seriously," Rosemary continued.

Nancy pricked up her ears at the information. Here was genuine news!

"Nathan Gombet!" she exclaimed. "What sort of an offer did he make you?"

"Oh, Gombet isn't honest," Floretta broke in feelingly. "We won't have anything to do with him any more. You see, he claimed we gave him an option to buy our house for six thousand dollars."

"Six thousand! Why, that's ridiculous. Surely, you didn't give such an option?"

"Mercy, no! But Gombet claims we did."

"The house is worth at least twenty thousand," Rosemary declared. "And if the city should decide to use it for a historical museum, we ought to get even more than that for it."

"I should think so," Nancy agreed. "Gombet was trying to cheat you."

"We never gave him any sort of option," Floretta insisted. "We wouldn't do business with him at any price, because we couldn't trust him. He would cheat us out of our eye teeth!"

"How long ago did all this happen?"

"Oh, it must have been nearly a year ago," Rosemary said, trying to recall. "It was last spring."

"The matter went to court?"

"No. Nathan Gombet threatened to make trouble and he said he would sue us, but nothing ever came of it."

"We had forgotten all about him until you brought up the subject," Floretta added.

"Then, have you heard nothing more from him since?"

"He threatened us once," Rosemary told Nancy. "Said he would make us sorry we hadn't sold at his price. But nothing ever came of the threat."

"How long ago was that?"

"Two or three months ago, I should judge."

Nancy Drew nodded thoughtfully and relapsed into deep meditation. She was now convinced that Nathan Gombet had some connection with the mysterious things which had been going on in the old house. Perhaps he was trying to frighten Rosemary and Floretta so that they would be glad to sell at his price.

"Gombet hasn't approached you with a new offer recently, has he?" she asked.

Floretta shook her head.

"We haven't seem him for some time, and we don't want to either."

"You don't think Gombet has had anything to do with what has happened lately, do you?" Rosemary questioned the girl.

"Of course I don't know, but I'm beginning to suspect there may be a connection," Nancy returned. "At least, I intend to investigate that line and see what it leads to."

"To be sure, there's nothing in Nathan Gombet's character that would prevent his using any underhand method to induce us to sell him this house," said Rosemary musingly. "Still, I don't see what opportunity he's had to do what's been done here. He hasn't been near us for some time, you know, Nancy."

"That's true," replied the girl. "But someone must have made the opportunity. Mr. Gombet has the motive and is so lacking in any sense of honor that would keep him from injuring you in this way, that I believe he furnishes the best lead to follow."

With that she left the bedroom and went to her own room farther down the hall. But as she sat by the window trying to think her way through the jumble of information she had gleaned, she found it difficult to keep her mind on the mystery.

After a time she took the crumpled telegram she had received earlier that morning from her pocket and studied it again. How could she interest herself in a mystery when her father was missing? What had happened to him? Oh, if only she could answer that question!

CHAPTER XIV

What Happened to Carson Drew

After taking leave of his daughter at the River Heights railroad station, Carson Drew boarded the Chicago train. Upon arriving in the city he lost no time in dispatching the business which had brought him to the great city on the lake. He had expected to remain in Chicago a full week, but so successful were his negotiations that his business was completed a day earlier than he had anticipated.

"I may as well send Nancy a telegram and return a day earlier," Mr. Drew decided.

Accordingly, he sent his daughter a message to the effect that he would arrive at the Cliffwood station the following morning. He then boarded the night flyer. He did not dream that the telegram would never reach Nancy. It was destined to fall into the hands of an enemy.

Oblivious of impending danger, Mr. Drew settled himself comfortably in the Pullman and took up a newspaper. The train had been moving perhaps an hour when the conductor came through and paused at his seat.

"Carson Drew?" he inquired.

"That's my name."

"Then here's a telegram for you. We picked it up at the last station."

Wonderingly, Mr. Drew accepted the envelope and quickly ripped it open. He smiled with pleasure as he read the message:

"Will meet you at the Cliffwood station.
"Nancy."

"Well, I'm glad to know she received my message," he thought, "though I didn't expect her to answer the telegram. I'm greatly relieved that nothing happened to her while I was in Chicago. Somehow, I didn't like the idea of letting her go off to that old stone house by herself. Anything might have happened."

Relieved that all was well with his daughter, Carson Drew settled himself to enjoy the evening paper. After reading it for perhaps an hour, he tossed it aside and went out to the observation car to give the porter an opportunity to make up his berth. After smoking a cigar he returned and before he retired left an order for the porter to call him in the morning.

In spite of the sway and rumble of the train, he slept soundly and did not open his eyes until the porter called him.

"Twenty minutes out of Cliffwood, suh."

Mr. Drew dressed himself hastily and prepared to get off at the station. He was eager to see Nancy again, for it seemed a month since he had been at home. It was nice of her to offer to meet him at such an early hour, he told himself. It was not yet seven o'clock.

The train came to a stop, and he swung from the step to the platform. Where was Nancy? Carson Drew glanced about in all directions, but his daughter was not in sight. Perhaps she had been delayed, he thought. Oh, well, no matter. He would wait a few minutes, and then if she failed to come along, he could call a taxi.

He picked up his bag and started toward the waiting room, but he had taken less than a dozen steps when he saw a man hurrying toward him. Carson Drew frowned as he saw who it was. He had no desire to meet Nathan Gombet. Undoubtedly, the man would try to argue with him again about his so-called property rights on the river.

"That fellow is a pest," Mr. Drew told himself. "Just my luck to run into him."

But as Nathan Gombet approached, he could not help but see that the man was laboring under great excitement.

"Wonder what's the matter with him now?" he asked himself curiously.

Nathan Gombet came straight toward him.

"Oh, Mr. Drew," he cried as he came up, "I have terrible news! Your daughter has been injured! You must come quickly!"

"Nancy is hurt?" Mr. Drew grasped him roughly by the arm. "It can't be!"

"She's badly injured. But the doctors think she has a chance to pull through."

"How horrible!" Carson Drew groaned.

"She's calling for you. You must come quickly!"

"Take me to her!"

In his anxiety to reach the daughter he loved so dearly, Carson Drew became almost frantic.

"Here, jump in!" Gombet ordered.

He opened the front door of a battered auto which stood near the platform. Mr. Drew, bewildered and shocked from the crushing news, obeyed without question.

Gombet scrambled in after him. He took the wheel and with one quick glance about started off down the street.

The station on this side was practically deserted and no one saw the car depart.

"Where is Nancy?" Mr. Drew demanded.

"At my house."

"At your house?" Mr. Drew asked, in surprise. "Didn't they take her to a hospital?"

"She was too badly injured to be moved," Nathan explained glibly.

"Oh, my poor little girl," Carson Drew murmured brokenly. A moment later he said: "You didn't tell me how she was hurt."

"In an automobile accident. Her roadster ran off into a ditch."

"And she was taken to your place?"

Mr. Drew did not like the look on Nathan Gombet's face. Was the man deceiving him? No, it was more likely he was trying to keep Nancy's true condition from him. Perhaps she had been so seriously injured that she was practically at the point of death. The thought nearly drove him wild.

"The accident occurred in front of my house," Gombet continued, trying to make his explanation appear plausible. "The doctor brought her inside."

"Oh, and Nancy was always such a safe driver, too."

"I didn't see the accident myself, but they say the steering gear broke."

"Tell me, will she live?"

"I can't tell you that."

The drive, though not a long one, seemed endless to Carson Drew. Nancy! His daughter! His little girl! The widowed father and the motherless girl were very close to each other. In what condition would he find her when he reached the end of this soul-trying drive? Was she conscious? Was she alive? He turned impatiently to Nathan Gombet.

"Hurry!" Mr. Drew urged. "I can't get there quickly enough!"

"The car won't go any faster," Gombet grunted.

And indeed it would not. Gombet was already driving as fast as he dared. Carson Drew was so worried that he asked no more questions but kept his eyes glued upon the road.

Gombet drove furiously and they soon reached the outskirts of Cliffwood. Presently they came within sight of two large stone houses, and Nathan Gombet turned in at one of them.

"I live here," he explained.

Carson Drew did not so much as give the house a casual glance. The instant the car stopped he sprang to the ground and started for the door. Quick as he was, Nathan Gombet was ahead of him. He opened the door for the lawyer and led the way through the kitchen where a fat, slovenly looking colored woman was working over the stove.

Had Mr. Drew not been intent upon reaching the bedside of his daughter, he would have observed that the colored woman received a significant nod from Nathan Gombet as he passed near her.

The moment the two men had passed into the next room, she walked over and quietly locked the outside door.

"This way," Nathan directed.

He opened a door and indicated a long, dark stairway. Without hesitation, Carson Drew followed him. He went up a flight of circular stairs and at last came to a landing.

Nathan paused and indicated a door to the left.

"Your daughter is in there," he said.

There was an eager, cruel gleam in his eyes, but Carson Drew did not notice.

"It won't frighten her for me to go right in?" the lawyer asked anxiously.

"No, it won't frighten her."

Hesitating no longer, Carson Drew opened the door and stepped inside. To his surprise the room was dark. The curtains were pulled down over the windows and at first he could see nothing. Then, as his eyes became accustomed to the darkness, he saw that he was not in a bedroom. The place had every appearance of a prison.

Carson Drew realized that he had walked into a trap.

He wheeled about and faced Nathan Gombet who stood in the doorway, eying him, gloating upon him.

"What does this mean?" he demanded sharply. "Where is Nancy?"

"It means that you are my prisoner," Gombet retorted, with an evil leer. "Before I get through with you I guess you'll come to terms about that property!"

With that he slammed the door shut and before Carson Drew could make a move turned the key in the lock. As the old miser trudged down the corridor, his hollow laughter echoed through the house.

CHAPTER XV

A Prisoner

As he heard the key turn in the lock, Carson Drew stood for a moment as though paralyzed. Things had happened so rapidly since he had left the train at the Cliffwood station that he could scarcely think logically. The fear that Nancy had been injured had driven everything else from his mind. Now he realized that all unwittingly he had walked into a trap.

Angrily, he jerked at the door, but it would not give. He kicked at it savagely, but after a few minutes was convinced that it could not be broken down even with a ram, for it was made of extra heavy wood. He did not cry out for help, for he realized that there was no one near who could aid him.

At last he sank down into a chair. What a fool he had been not to suspect a plot! It was all clear to him now. Undoubtedly, Gombet had intercepted the telegram which he had sent to Nancy, or in some way had learned of the lawyer's intended visit to Cliffwood. He had lied about Nancy in order to induce him to come to this house.

"I don't care what Nathan does to me, if only Nancy is safe," Carson Drew thought.

What had become of her? He did not believe she had been hurt as Nathan had stated, but it was possible that the miser had taken her prisoner also.

Nervously, Carson Drew paced the floor. The room was dark, but as his eyes became accustomed to it, he noticed a small window far above. The window was heavily barred.

"Evidently this room was fitted up for a prison," he told himself grimly. "I imagine Nathan Gombet has been biding his time to get me here."

There was little furniture in the room—nothing but a cot, a table, and a chair. Mr. Drew pulled the table across the room and by standing on it was able to look out of the window.

The courtyard was far below, and one glance disclosed the fact that even if it were possible to break the bars, he could not hope to escape. It would be suicide to drop to the ground, and there was no tree or building near by.

"Nathan thought of everything," Carson Drew observed dryly. "He has me completely at his mercy."

Just what Gombet would do with him, Mr.

Drew did not know, but he suspected the miser would go to any length to gain his end.

"I'll never give in to him!" he resolved firmly.

Presently, glancing out of the window again, he noticed a stone house some distance away which appeared not unlike the one in which he was imprisoned.

"Can that be the Turnbull house?" he questioned himself.

He tried to recall the description Nancy had given him, and every detail tallied. He was convinced that the stone house was indeed The Mansion.

"I wonder if Nancy is still there?" flashed through his mind. "Oh, if only she returns to River Heights before that fiend gets his hands on her!" It was characteristic of Carson Drew to think of his daughter's safety before his own. She was always first.

As the hours dragged slowly on, he kept a close watch of the neighboring house, hoping to catch a glimpse of Nancy or someone to whom he could signal. At noon the colored woman appeared with his luncheon, which consisted of bread and water, shoved through a small hole at the bottom of the door. Mr. Drew drank the water but did not touch the bread.

All afternoon he maintained his watch at the

tiny window. The Turnbull home appeared deserted. What had become of Nancy? Had she already departed, or was she, too, held a prisoner at the hands of Gombet?

Toward evening, Carson Drew was startled to hear heavy footsteps in the corridor. He scrambled down from the window, but there was not enough time to move the table back into place.

Nathan Gombet stepped into the room. Carefully locking the door, he placed an oil lamp on the table and gave Carson Drew a gloating grin.

"How do you like it here by this time?" he asked with elaborate politeness.

"Oh, it's very pleasant," Mr. Drew returned sarcastically. "You may as well put your cards on the table, Nathan Gombet. What do you want of me?"

Nathan became intently eager.

"You know what I want," he muttered. "You must pay me for my land and sign a paper that you will not prosecute. If you will do that, I'll let you go free."

"Indeed?"

"Yes," Nathan smiled gleefully. "I want a check for twenty thousand dollars. And if you know what's wise, you'll hand it over without batting an eyelash."

Carson Drew smiled grimly.

"You old reprobate! You'll never get a cent!"

While he had been talking, Mr. Drew had done fast thinking. Now, he made a sudden spring toward Nathan Gombet, intending to overpower him. Quick as the action was, the old miser was prepared. Taking a step backwards, he deliberately pulled a gun upon the lawyer.

"Oh, no, you don't," he snarled. "And just for that trick I'm going to tie you up!"

Still covering Mr. Drew with the revolver and never taking his eyes from the lawyer's face, Gombet cautiously backed up to the door and unlocked it. The heavy-set colored woman whom Mr. Drew had seen in the kitchen came into the room so quickly that it was obvious she had been standing just outside the door ready to aid the miser when summoned.

"Tie him up!" Nathan ordered harshly.

"Yes, suh."

The colored woman disappeared, to return in a few minutes with heavy ropes. As she waddled across the floor she clumsily brushed against Nathan and entangled one of his feet in the rope.

"Take care what you're doing," the miser reprimanded her sharply.

He gave the rope a savage kick, and then emitted a howl of pain.

"Tarnation, but that leg does hurt," he muttered. "Fell on a broken stair step and just about killed myself. Leg's pained me ever since!" He wheeled upon the colored woman as though she were responsible for his misfortune, but without ceasing to cover Carson Drew with the revolver. "Get a move on there! Tie that man up and be quick about it!"

"Yes, suh."

Sullenly, the colored woman set herself to the task. With the pistol staring him in the face, the lawyer dared not resist. He was pushed roughly into a chair and securely bound to it with the heavy ropes.

"Now how do you like it?" Nathan Gombet demanded, with satisfaction, when the task had been completed.

Carson Drew did not give him the pleasure of an answer.

"Now, will you come to my terms?"

"I will not!"

Nathan stared at the lawyer in disbelief. He had not believed that Mr. Drew would dare defy him.

"That's your final decision?"

"It is."

"You'll be glad enough to come to my terms when I get through with you, Carson Drew!"

"Do your worst." Carson Drew smiled provokingly. Then his eyes narrowed. "But remember this. You'll be brought to justice in the end, and when you are, the law won't be lenient with you!"

"The law!" Gombet laughed scornfully. "A lot of good it will ever do you! You'll never see your daughter or your friends again unless you give me the money. Will you sign the papers?"

"I've given you your answer. Can't you understand plain English?"

"All right, I've given you your last chance!" Nathan's face became convulsed with rage. "In a day or so you'll be glad enough to do as I ask. I'll starve you to it!"

Carson Drew shrugged his shoulders indifferently. Nathan Gombet saw that his threat had made little impression upon the lawyer.

"And if that ain't enough to bring you to time," he added with a wicked laugh. "I'll get your daughter here, too!"

A look of horror came into Mr. Drew's eyes.

"You couldn't do that! Why, you don't even know where she is!"

"Oh, don't I? She's right at the Turnbulls' house. I can get her here easily any night. Just have to dope her a bit, that's all."

"You fiend!" Carson Drew struggled at his bonds, but he was helpless.

Nathan Gombet laughed again, and turned toward the door.

"No more food or water for you," he called back, as he turned to leave.

Carson Drew heard the key turn in the lock, and then he was left to sober reflection. He did not doubt that Nathan Gombet would attempt to carry out his ugly threat. That night he might enter The Mansion and abduct Nancy. The thought made him ill.

"What can I do?" he asked himself miserably. "Perhaps, after all, I had better do as Nathan asks."

CHAPTER XVI

A New Clue

For two days after the arrival of the telegram from Chicago which stated that Carson Drew had left for home, Nancy waited hopefully. But as the time passed and no word was received from her father, her anxiety intensified. All sorts of unpleasant thoughts began to trouble her.

Had her father met with an accident? Perhaps, in crossing the street, he had been struck by an automobile. Oh, if only he would come or send word of his whereabouts! The suspense was almost unendurable.

At the repeated urging of Rosemary and Floretta, she consented to remain at The Mansion until she received news from her father. But the strain of waiting was beginning to tell heavily upon her. Since Carson Drew had left River Heights, she had not even received a letter from him.

Nancy's interest in the mystery of the old stone house gradually lessened. She was still determined to solve the enigma, but the fear that something had happened to her father overshadowed all else.

Since the theft of the silk dresses from Floretta's room, nothing had happened to disturb the tranquillity of the Turnbull household, although an atmosphere of suspense seemed to hover over the entire house. Sometimes Nancy thought that the very silence of the place would drive her into hysterics. She longed to depart, but for the sake of Floretta and Rosemary she remained.

Several times she had searched the house in the hope of finding secret openings in the walls, but although when she rapped them a few had a hollow sound, she was never able to find any hidden door. It was discouraging.

Since Nancy had learned that Nathan Gombet was endeavoring to purchase the Turnbull mansion at a ridiculously low price, she felt that she had struck a valuable clue. In her own mind she was firmly convinced that the miser had some connection with the strange things which had been going on in the old house. She had no way of establishing the identity of the thief, but she was certain that it was either Gombet or someone employed by him.

"He intends to scarce Rosemary and Floretta into selling at any price," Nancy thought. "It's up to me to quench his little game!"

She was at a loss to know what course to follow. If only her father were there to give her advice!

"As a last resort I'll go to Gombet and have a talk with him," she decided. "By skillful questioning I may be able to learn something which will incriminate him."

Nancy was well aware that Nathan Gombet was clever as well as scheming. It would be difficult to convict him of entering The Mansion, that she knew. She could not cause him to be arrested upon suspicion.

"I must find a way to prove that he is the guilty one," she thought. "If I delay too long, something terrible may happen here. That miser is a desperate man when crossed."

Convinced that it was unwise to postpone her visit to the home of the miser, she determined to visit him that very day, although she dreaded the ordeal.

"Can you tell me where Nathan Gombet lives?" she asked Rosemary at the luncheon table.

"Why, don't you know?" Rosemary asked. "He lives in the old stone house directly back of us."

Nancy gave an exclamation of surprise.

"I wish I had known that before."

"We would have mentioned it, but we thought you knew."

"You think Gombet has something to do with the mystery?" Floretta questioned curiously.

"I'm almost certain of it. But to prove my theory will not be easy. Nathan is as clever as he is scheming. Tell me, how long has he lived in the stone house?"

"Oh, for years. And a mighty unpleasant neighbor he is, too."

"I can imagine," and Nancy smiled grimly.

"You see, there's quite a story connected with Nathan's ownership of the house," Floretta began. "Would you care to hear it?"

"Indeed, I would."

"The house was originally built by a Turnbull. That explains why it so closely resembles our own."

"Both homes were built by the same man?" Nancy asked.

"No; by two brothers." It was Rosemary who answered. "They were devoted to each other, and for that reason they built their houses close together, although, as you can see, they are on different roads."

"When the Civil War broke out, the brothers had their first disagreement," Floretta continued the story. "William, the brother who owned this house, was a staunch supporter of the Union, but the other brother joined the Confederate forces."

"He gave his life as well as his fortune to the cause," Rosemary broke in.

"He was killed in action," Floretta finished. "After his death it was learned that he had heavily mortgaged his home. Everything went to pay the debts. The house passed from one person to another until finally it fell into the hands of Nathan Gombet."

"But why does he want to buy your home?" Nancy demanded, with a puzzled frown. "If he hopes to sell to the city, why doesn't he give up his own house."

"The city doesn't want it," Rosemary explained. "He did try to sell. His house doesn't have as interesting a history as ours does, and he has permitted it to run down. It's in a terrible condition now. I shouldn't be surprised any day to see it tumble from its foundation."

"Nathan has always been queer," Floretta remarked. "As long as we can remember he has lived alone."

"Not exactly alone," Rosemary broke in. "He keeps a servant. A colored woman who looks as though she were an ogre."

"And birds," Floretta added. "His house fairly swarms with them. When they die, he stuffs them! Ug!" She shuddered. "You couldn't hire me to go near his place."

"You say he keeps birds?" Nancy inquired, with quickening interest. "What kind?"

"Oh, most every kind, I guess," Rosemary answered. "Parrots. You can hear them screeching clear over here sometimes."

"Does he keep canaries?" Nancy questioned eagerly.

"Oh, yes," Rosemary agreed.

The significance of the question did not dawn upon Rosemary and Floretta, and Nancy did not tell them what was in her mind. At once she had thought of the two canaries which had found their way into The Mansion so mysteriously. Was it not likely that Nathan Gombet had brought the birds from his own home? But how had he succeeded in entering the mansion without being discovered? That question remained unanswered.

"I must visit the other house without delay," she told herself. "But how can I manage it? If I openly call upon Mr. Gombet he's certain to suspect my purpose and perhaps hold me a prisoner."

If only she could find a way to enter the house without Nathan's knowledge!

"I'll keep a close watch on the house, and I may see him leave," she decided. "If I do —that will be my chance."

Nancy was excited at the information which she had secured, and was eager for action. She felt that the solution to the mystery was almost within her grasp.

She laid her plans carefully. She refrained from telling Rosemary and Floretta of her intention to visit Gombet's house, for she knew they would be afraid to permit her to attempt the dangerous mission.

"If conditions are right, I'll slip away this very night," she resolved.

All that afternoon she moved restlessly about the house, making frequent trips to the window to glance searchingly toward the old stone dwelling which was half-hidden by tall trees.

"Time never dragged more slowly," Nancy complained. "I wish night would come."

She ate little dinner, for as the hour approached, she realized more keenly than before that she was about to undertake a dangerous adventure. Clouds had been forming in the sky all afternoon, and by the time the shadows began to gather a drizzly rain had set in. Nothing could have pleased her more.

"What a horrible night," Floretta remarked nervously as she glanced at the rain-splashed windows. "I hope we don't have another visit from our ghost. It's just the sort of night for something to happen."

Rosemary looked displeased at this audible expression of her sister's nervousness.

Nancy smiled reassuringly.

"I have a feeling that this is going to be an unlucky night for our ghost," she said evenly. "And now, if you will excuse me, I believe I'll retire early."

After saying good night to Rosemary and Floretta, Nancy Drew went directly to her room. But she did not prepare for bed. On this night she had an important mission ahead of her.

CHAPTER XVII

Under Cover of Darkness

Nancy Drew dressed herself in garments that would resist the rain, and then removed her flashlight and pistol from their hiding places. The latter she examined carefully to make certain it was loaded and ready for instant use.

"I may need it to-night," she assured herself grimly. "No telling what I'll get into."

Nancy was in a hurry to get away, and it seemed that the Turnbull sisters were never going to bed. Presently, she heard them moving about downstairs and knew they were locking up for the night. After an interminable wait, they came upstairs and went into their respective rooms. A half hour more, and the house was quiet.

"Now is my chance," Nancy thought. "If only I can get out of here without being heard."

Hastily slipping into her slicker and pulling a tight-fitting turban over her curly, bobbed hair, she picked up her flashlight and revolver. She opened the bedroom door and listened. All was quiet.

"I feel like a ghost myself," Nancy chuckled, as she tiptoed past Rosemary's room.

The floor creaked alarmingly, and she paused, fearful lest she had awakened the Turnbull sisters. She did not wish to frighten them and neither did she wish to explain why she was prowling about at such a late hour.

Apparently the noise had not been heard, for no sound issued from either bedroom. Rosemary and Floretta were both sleeping soundly. After hesitating a moment, Nancy cautiously crept on down the stairway.

She groped her way down the steps and upon reaching the drawing room, turned on the flashlight. Quietly, she made her way to the front door. As she had expected, it was locked.

She felt for the key, but did not find it. Surprised, she flashed her light full upon the lock. The key was not there.

"Just my luck," she murmured. "Rosemary and Floretta must have hidden it somewhere."

Softly, she moved through the house to the kitchen and tried the back door. It also was locked and the key likewise was missing.

"Now I am in a nice mess," Nancy told herself in disgust. "There's no hope of ever finding the key. I'll have to go through a window."

Rosemary and Floretta had not forgotten to lock the windows, but they had been barred from the inside, and the one in the kitchen offered little resistance when Nancy tried it. Quietly raising it, she crawled through and pushed it down when she had reached the ground.

The rain was falling steadily, and a sudden gust of wind blew a wet spray into her face. She did not mind. The blacker and stormier the night, the more effectively it would serve her purpose.

She did not light her flashlight for fear of attracting attention to her movements. Splashing through the mud and water, she tried to pierce the darkness. She could see only a short way ahead, but she knew the exact location of the other house, and headed for it. Her heart began to beat faster as she contemplated the adventure before her. If all went as she planned, she hoped to solve the mystery of the Turnbull mansion before she returned.

As the outlines of the other stone house gradually emerged from the murkiness of the drizzly night, she experienced a sensation of dread. The night's work was not going to be pleasant, of that she was sure.

There was something about the house which seemed sinister. Through the mistlike rain, the rays of a light in one of the lower rooms shone forth as if in a half-futile attempt to pierce the gloom, while the rest of the house stood dark and somber.

So this was the home of Nathan Gombet, Nancy ruminated. She could not help but feel that the dark, uninviting aspect of the structure provided an abode singularly in keeping with the sinister character of its master.

As she stood in the shadow of the tall maples which surrounded the house, she was uncertain what course it would be wisest to follow. She did not wish to blunder into danger and she especially dreaded an encounter with Nathan Gombet. Yet, if she accomplished anything, she must enter the house, and it must be done this night.

She squared her shoulders and stepped forward. At that very moment the front door of the dwelling opened. Startled, Nancy retreated behind a tree.

A man came out of the house. Unmindful of the rain, he stood for several minutes with his face turned in the direction of the Turnbull mansion.

It was Nathan Gombet.

Nancy recognized him as the light from the window shone full upon his face and clearly defined his features. The stoop of his shoulders was unmistakable.

She crouched behind a tree and waited. What did the miser intend to do? Perhaps he was contemplating another visit to the Turnbull mansion! Otherwise, why would he stand there and stare in that direction?

Nancy could not know that Nathan was deliberately planning a scheme which boded ill for her. The old miser had just ended a stormy interview with Carson Drew who was held prisoner in the tower room of the house, and he had made up his mind to bring the lawyer to time by kidnapping his daughter. Just how he would get his hands on Nancy he did not know, but as he abruptly started off down the path, he was turning over a number of plans in his head.

"The time will soon be ripe," he chuckled evilly.

Unaware that Nathan had been thinking of her and likewise without a suspicion that she stood within a stone's throw of the room where her father was imprisoned, Nancy Drew considered what she had best do.

"There's not much use to trail Nathan," she decided. "After all, he may not visit the Turnbull house, and this will be my only opportunity to visit his house. It was pure luck he left just when he did."

Hesitating no longer, she moved on through the rain. Once she glanced back over her shoulder, but Nathan Gombet had been swallowed up in the darkness.

Cautiously, Nancy approached the old stone house from the rear. The light was still shining from a window, and she saw now that it came from the kitchen. The shades were up, and as she drew closer she was able to peer in.

A fat colored woman was washing dishes at the sink, her back to the window.

"She must be the servant Rosemary and Floretta were telling me about," Nancy guessed. "I never saw a more surly-looking creature. She looks positively vicious!"

Nancy Drew was disappointed, for with Nathan Gombet gone she had hoped to find the house deserted. The presence of the colored woman made her mission a very dangerous one.

"It's now or never," she thought nervously. "I must hurry or Nathan Gombet may return."

Cautiously, she moved forward and surveyed the house at close range. With the exception of the kitchen, the shades were pulled down over all of the windows.

"I may be able to get in a cellar window," Nancy reasoned.

With one eye on the kitchen door, she began an investigation. After trying several windows, she found one which had not been locked.

"Luck is with me," she breathed. "Now, if I can get into the house without being detected!"

The window was a small one and swung back on a hinge. It made a loud grating sound as it opened, and Nancy felt certain the colored woman must have heard the noise. Frantically, she scrambled through the small opening and dropped to the cellar floor. Before she could prevent it, the window banged shut behind her.

"Now I have done it!" she thought, in a panic.

Her fears were confirmed. The kitchen door opened and there was a heavy tread on the back porch. The colored woman had heard the noise and was coming to find what had caused it.

CHAPTER XVIII

Inside the Other House

Nancy Drew crouched in the dark cellar of the old stone house, scarcely daring to breathe lest her presence be discovered. She could hear the old colored servant coming down the path which led directly to the window through which she had just scrambled.

"She heard the noise all right, and she's coming to investigate," Nancy thought fearfully.

She dared not turn on her flashlight to search for a hiding place and she dared not remain where she was. If the colored woman looked in at the window, as she was almost certain to do, her presence would be detected.

Feeling her way in the dark, Nancy moved cautiously forward. She could not see a foot ahead of her, and the cellar was unpleasantly musty and damp.

Her hand touched something cold and slimy. She recoiled as though she had touched a snake, although in reality it was only an old piece of rubber hose.

She could hear the colored woman coming nearer and nearer. Unless she found a hiding place quickly, she would be caught.

Then her hand touched a doorknob. She turned it eagerly. The door opened readily, and Nancy found herself in a small storeroom.

There was no time to search for a better place, so she quickly drew the door to after her. Leaving a tiny crack through which she could peep, she waited anxiously.

Almost immediately, she heard a noise at the cellar window, and a light was flashed about. It rested for a moment upon the door of the storeroom and then moved to another corner.

"I suah thought I heard somethin'!" Nancy heard the old negress mutter. "An' it was right down in this heah basement, too!"

She continued to flash the long beam of her flashlight here and there about the cellar, and though Nancy could see nothing at the window because of the glare, she imagined that back of the lens she saw two penetrating black eyes peering directly into her retreat.

"If she sees me!" Nancy thought, and the prospect of being captured like a thief in the house of Nathan Gombet caused her to crouch closely to the wall, praying that the colored woman would not discover her. "If she decides to come down into the cellar, I'm lost," she told herself.

Apparently, the colored woman was satisfied that there was nothing wrong in the basement, for after peering in at the window, she moved away, muttering to herself.

"I done reckons my old ears is playin' me false," she mumbled. "I hears noises dat sounds like dey was in de basement and dey was only in my haid."

A moment later Nancy heard the kitchen door slam shut. After waiting several minutes longer to make certain that the old colored woman had no intention of returning, she switched on her flashlight and curiously surveyed her surroundings.

The storeroom in which she found herself was like any other room of its kind, though it showed neglect. The place was filthy with dirt, and in one corner some half-rotten potatoes sent up an odor which was anything but pleasant.

After assuring herself that there was nothing of interest in the room, Nancy opened the door and quietly stepped out into the main part of the basement. It was a relief to get a whiff of comparatively fresh air.

Her purpose in entering the cellar was to discover whether or not there was a secret tunnel connecting the Turnbull mansion with Nathan Gombet's house. Since she had learned that both residences had been built at approximately the same time, she had suspected that such a passageway might be in existence. She had been unable to find an entrance in the cellar of the Turnbull mansion, but she hoped to have better luck in the basement of Gombet's house.

Flashing her light over the walls, she searched diligently for a secret opening or a trapdoor. Obviously, there was no tunnel which opened out of the basement. The walls appeared to be constructed of solid stone.

However, as she moved her light about, she saw a flight of stairs which led to the first floor of the house.

Nancy Drew had no intention of leaving the place until she had made a thorough investigation of the floors above, but the stairway she had located led directly into the kitchen. So long as the colored woman was working there, she would be held a prisoner in the cellar.

"I may have to wait here until she goes to bed," she thought dismally.

A girl less patient would have given up the search, but Nancy was determined to see the affair through to the end. Unless she here and now unearthed an important clue which would definitely connect Nathan Gombet with the strange happenings and numerous thefts at the Turnbull mansion, she feared that the mystery would forever remain unsolved.

She had visited the home of Gombet as a last

resort. She was firm in her intention not to return without the evidence which must be obtained before the old miser could be convicted.

The cellar was damp and Nancy's slicker was but slight protection against the chill night air. Presently, she was shivering with cold.

"This will never do," she chattered. "I can't stay here all night."

Discomfort made her bold. Impulsively, she crept up the stairway. A door blocked the entrance to the kitchen. Crouching down, she peered through the keyhole. The colored woman was still there. She stood with her back to the basement door, ironing.

It was slightly warmer on the landing and Nancy remained there, hoping that some errand would take the woman from the room. After what seemed an interminable wait, the negress put her ironing board away and, picking up the basket of clothes, went out of the kitchen.

Throwing caution to the winds, Nancy gently tried the door. It was not locked. Without making a sound, she opened it and stepped out into the light.

Now that she was actually in the kitchen she did not know which way to turn. As she hesitated, she heard the colored woman returning.

Frantically, Nancy glanced this way and that. There was not sufficient time to retreat to the cellar. The woman had nearly reached the kitchen.

"I'm trapped," the girl thought desperately.

Then her eyes rested upon a closet door to her left, and with scarcely an instant's consideration, she hastily sought the refuge it afforded.

Scarcely had she stepped into the closet and closed the door when the colored woman came back into the kitchen. Without so much as a glance in the direction of the closet, she picked up a pile of ironed linen and again left the room. Nancy could hear her moving about in another part of the house.

"Now is my chance!" she advised herself. "If I stay here I'll be sure to be caught."

Quickly, she stepped out of the closet. She listened for a second to make certain the woman was not returning, and then, without making a sound, darted into the next room.

There was no time to look about, for at any moment the colored woman might come back and find her there. She must reach the second floor. Where was the stairway?

Softly, she tiptoed across the floor and opened a door. Fortune favored her, for it was the right one. A narrow, winding stairway, not unlike the one in the Turnbull house, led to the landing above.

With her pistol ready for instant use, Nancy

Drew crept noiselessly up the stairs. The boards creaked slightly but she did not pause until she had reached the landing. It was pitch dark and she dared not use her flashlight.

She heard a noise, and started.

"That sounded like someone coughing, but I guess it couldn't have been," she decided. "My nerves are all on edge to-night."

Had she only known it, she stood within twenty feet of the room where her father was held a prisoner!

Nancy paused and listened, but the sound was not repeated.

She then crept silently along the corridor, unwittingly passing the prison chamber in the dark.

The floor boards creaked alarmingly, and at each step she feared someone would spring out and attempt to overpower her. She felt as though unseen eyes were watching her every movement.

"I must control my nerves," she told herself firmly.

By a supreme effort of will she gained control over herself and moved forward again. Her hand struck a door knob. Cautiously, she opened the door, wondering what would be revealed. In the inky blackness she could see nothing, and with sudden daring, switched on her flashlight.

As a penetrating beam fell upon an object directly in front of her, she started back in sheer horror.

A big owl, with spread wings and wicked glassy eyes, was less than three feet from her!

Only by rigid mental discipline did Nancy suppress a cry of fright. Then, as she continued to stare at the huge bird, she relaxed slightly.

The owl was stuffed! For a moment she had forgotten that Rosemary and Floretta had told her that Nathan Gombet was something of a taxidermist.

With misgiving, she flashed her light about. What she saw did not tend to lessen her terror. She stood in a room of birds!

"What a strange hobby," Nancy shuddered.

Never had she seen such a collection. The room was crowded with pedestals upon which sat stuffed birds. From one corner, an eagle looked down upon her, and from another, an ugly vulture. There were several crows and odd specimens Nancy did not recognize.

It was a gruesome sight. She stared at the figures in fascination and horror, for in the semi-darkness a score of glassy eyes seemed focused upon her.

Nancy's first impulse was to back hastily from the room, but almost immediately she gained control of herself. She would not leave until she had discovered every secret of the old house!

As she moved her light about, she saw that there were live birds in the room also. Golden canaries in gilded cages! They seemed strangely out of keeping with the ugly stuffed specimens about the walls and upon the pedestals. There were dozens of the little yellow birds, and as a beam from the flashlight struck the cages, they aroused sleepily on their perches and began to chirp and twitter.

"Canaries!" Nancy whispered, impressed at the sight. "Now I am sure it was Nathan Gombet who entered the Turnbull mansion. The two canaries which we found in Floretta's room must have come from here! But how did they get there? That is what I must find out before I leave here to-night!"

She turned toward the door and as she moved forward a ray from the flashlight fell upon a large cage which had escaped her notice. Now for the first time she saw a brilliantly colored parrot.

The bird began to stir restlessly. Sensing that she was about to bring disaster upon herself, Nancy switched the light to another portion of the room. Too late! The parrot let out a loud squawk.

"Go 'way!" it screamed. "Go 'way! Polly wants a cracker!"

Thoroughly alarmed, Nancy darted toward the door. As she opened the door, she heard a heavy step on the stairs. The colored woman was coming to find out what the matter was! Escape was cut off.

"I could choke that parrot!" Nancy told herself almost fiercely. "Now I am in a mess!"

CHAPTER XIX

A Chance Discovery

Softly, Nancy Drew closed the door. One quick glance toward the stairway had convinced her that she could not hope to escape into the corridor. Already the old colored woman, oil lamp in hand, had nearly reached the landing. Fortunately, she was fat and awkward and could not move swiftly. Nancy was thankful for that.

The ill-tempered parrot which had been the cause of all the trouble, was now fully awakened. It began to flutter about angrily in its cage and to squawk louder than before.

"Go 'way! Go 'way!" it screeched shrilly, cocking its head and eying her slyly.

"Oh, hush up, you horrid bird!" Nancy murmured in an undertone, as she scowled at the bird. "You've caused enough trouble as it is!"

She flashed her light about the room in a desperate attempt to find a hiding place. The room was bare of furniture.

She rushed to the window and glanced hopefully out. There was no ledge, and the drop to the ground would be suicide.

Nancy realized that she had never been in a more dangerous situation. She did not doubt that the old colored woman was as unscrupulous as her master, and what she would do if she found a stranger prowling in the house, Nancy dreaded to consider. At least she would turn her over to Nathan Gombet when he returned, and Nancy could think of no worse fate.

Nervously, she gripped her revolver. If the necessity arose, could she defend herself? She had never shot a firearm in her life at anything but a target, and she knew that she could never bring herself to the point of injuring a human being deliberately, even to save herself from capture. Yet, the revolver would serve as a bluff, and perhaps as an effective one.

"I can't afford to be caught here," she thought. "Even if I managed to escape it would put an end to my investigation, and I haven't learned half enough yet!"

In her prior survey of the bird room, Nancy had failed to notice a closet door directly behind the parrot's cage. Now, as her eyes turned again in that direction, she saw it for the first time.

With a low exclamation of pleasure and belief, she glided toward it. Opening the door, she stepped inside and closed it after her.

She was not an instant too soon, for scarcely had she entered the dark recess when she heard the room door open. The colored woman came waddling into the room. She flashed her light into the corners of the room and looked about in a puzzled manner as though unable to understand what had caused the commotion of the birds.

"Go 'way! Go 'way!" the parrot cackled, harping on its eternal theme. "Polly wants a cracker."

"How comes you so excited to-night, talkbird?" the woman demanded crossly. "You carries on like a fool with all yo' squawkin' and speechifyin'!"

"Go 'way! Go 'way!" the parrot repeated mechanically, fluttering its wings and swinging saucily on its cage trapeze.

"Oh, nev' mind, nev' mind!" the negress grunted. "I'll go 'way all right, but befo' I goes I's gwine cut off yo' conversation!"

Provoked that the bird had caused her to make a special trip upstairs, she picked up a piece of heavy canvas from the floor and flung it over the parrot's cage.

"I reckon dat'll hold you fo' a spell!" she muttered.

The parrot gave a last dismal squawk and then became quiet.

The woman stood beside the bird cage regarding it with satisfaction. She was not more than a yard or two from the closet door and if she had reached out her hand could have touched the handle.

Fearful lest she be discovered, Nancy pressed herself again the wall of the closet and remained motionless. She felt a tiny little knob pressing uncomfortably into the hollow of her back, but without a light she could not see what it was. Later, if she escaped detection, she intended to investigate.

Now, she knew that the slightest noise would bring the enemy down upon her in an instant. For some reason, the colored woman showed an inclination to remain even after she had covered the bird cage. Perhaps she sensed a foreign presence in the room. At all events she stood near the closet, listening.

The room was silent save for the twittering of the canaries. Nancy held her breath in suspense. Would she be discovered? It was a nerve-wracking moment.

Again the woman flashed her light about the room, but she did not turn toward the closet. After a last careful look around, she moved heavily toward the door. There she paused and appeared to reflect.

"Cain't make out what upset that there bird all of a sudden," she said to herself. "Reckons I ain't gwine take no chances."

With that, she went out and closed the door behind her. Nancy heard a peculiar grating sound, but was at a loss to explain it.

The colored woman shuffled down the corridor and as she descended the stairs to the lower floor, her footsteps gradually died away. After waiting several minutes, Nancy emerged from her hiding place. The air had become unpleasantly stuffy within the closet, and she was glad to get out.

Avoiding the parrot cage, she crept noiselessly to the door. She grasped the knob and pulled, but to her astonishment the door did not open. Again she tried, but without success.

The door was locked!

Now Nancy comprehended the significance of the peculiar grating noise she had heard directly after the negress had left the room. It was the sound of a key turning in the lock. She, Nancy Drew, was a prisoner in the bird room—the "chamber of horrors."

"Now what shall I do?" Nancy questioned herself miserably. "Oh, why did I ever come to this horrible place, anyway?"

She sank down on the floor and tried to think of a way out of the predicament, but could not. Her zest for adventure had been her undoing.

"If I ever get out of here alive I'll think twice before I go blundering into anything like this again," she promised herself.

Presently, she walked over to the window and glanced toward the Turnbull mansion. If only she could wish herself safely back into her own room!

"And the worst part of it is that I haven't discovered what I came to find out," she mourned. "I'm sure there is a secret panel in this house, but now I'll never find it. I'm certain it wouldn't be in this room."

Because there was nothing else to do, she began a half-hearted examination of the walls. As she had expected, she found nothing of interest. She was about to give up in disgust when a sudden thought came to her.

She recalled the knob she had felt within the closet. Probably it was nothing, but at least it would do no harm to have a look at it.

Flashing her light into the closet, she focused it upon the knob in question. It was a tiny thing and appeared to have no special purpose. Certainly it was not the right size to serve as an object upon which to hang clothing.

"I wonder what it is for?" the girl asked herself.

Curiously, Nancy stepped inside the closet and twisted the knob. She thought she heard a clicking noise. Was it only imagination?

Eagerly, she examined the back wall of the closet and her interest quickened. In the dim light she could make out a long crack. She tapped the wall with her knuckles, and it had a hollow sound.

"I believe I've stumbled upon something important," Nancy thought excitedly.

With all her might she pushed upon the knob. Unexpectedly, a spring clicked and the entire side of the closet wall dropped down!

Nancy struggled to maintain her balance, but could not. She toppled forward and fell headlong down a steep flight of stone steps.

A low cry of pain escaped her, and then she lay still.

CHAPTER XX

The Underground Passage

After Nancy Drew had plunged through the opening into the dark abyss, the closet wall clapped back into place. She did not hear the spring click, for before she reached the bottom of a long flight of stone stairs her head struck a hard object and she lost consciousness.

For several minutes she remained in a limp little heap at the bottom of the stairs. When at last she opened her eyes, she gave a little moan of pain, and tried to recollect what had happened.

She could see nothing, for she was enveloped in darkness. Gradually, she began to recall the events leading up to the sudden fall through the opening in the wall. She could remember pressing the tiny knob in the closet, but there her memory failed her. Evidently, she had found the secret panel and was now in an underground chamber.

As yet, Nancy was too badly shaken to realize the full importance of the discovery. She sat up and gingerly felt of her head. There was a big bump over her left eye.

"Lucky I wasn't killed," she murmured.

She scrambled slowly to her feet and moved first one limb and then another. She had been sorely bruised and scratched in the fall, but so far as she could tell no bones were broken.

In the descent she had lost both her revolver and flashlight, and she began to grope around in the dark, hoping to find them.

She found the revolver almost at her feet, but it required a diligent search before her hand struck the flashlight. It had lodged in a corner near the last step.

"I hope it isn't broken," she thought anxiously, as she picked it up.

To her relief, the flashlight had not been damaged. When she turned it on it worked perfectly, but its feeble light illuminated only a small portion of the surroundings.

Nancy saw that she had fallen to the very bottom of a long stone stairway. In vain she looked for the opening through which she had plunged. It had vanished as though by magic.

"That's strange," she murmured, bewildered. "I know I fell down those steps."

Limping painfully up the stairs, she stared in astonishment at the solid wall at the top. She ran her hands up and down but could not find the hidden spring.

"Oh, well, I could probably find it if I hunted long enough," she told herself. "But I'm only wasting valuable time. I've found the secret passage at last, and, the Fates being willing, I intend to find out where it leads. I can investigate this panel later when I have more time."

Nancy cautiously descended into the tunnel. The steps were of crudely cut stone and led almost straight down into an inky, uncertain blackness. Beyond, stretched a passageway.

When she reached the bottom of the steps, she paused, undecided what to do. She did not know where the passage might lead; she might be walking into danger.

"I'll chance it," she decided. "I wouldn't turn back for anything in the world now."

The passageway which stretched uninvitingly before her was very narrow and only high enough for her to walk without bending over. The sides were built of brick and stone, but the material had begun to crumble and Nancy feared that at any moment a portion of the walls or ceiling might come tumbling down upon her.

"Well, here's for it," she decided resolutely.

She moved slowly forward, flashing her light ahead of her. The passage was unpleasantly damp and had an earthy smell. Moisture clung to the walls, and there was a cold breeze circulating.

"I must be underground," she thought.

An awful silence reigned in the subterranean passage. The quiet was oppressive. With an anxious glance over her shoulder, Nancy went on.

Once she thought she heard a sigh from someone in distress. Involuntarily, she stopped to listen.

"I guess it was only the wind," she told herself uncertainly.

On she went deeper into the labyrinth of darkness, feeling her way cautiously. The tiny light from her flashlight but dimly illuminated the passage, and she stumbled and groped her way along timidly. When she accidentally brushed against the stone walls or put out a hand to save herself from falling, the structure felt clammy and repulsive to the touch.

"Silly!" she chided herself sternly.

But in spite of her determination, she could not free her mind from unpleasant supposition. The gruesome sights she had seen in the bird room had made an unpleasant impression upon her. What if the colored woman had heard her fall down the stairs and knew the secret of the hidden panel in the closet? At this very moment she might be following.

Nancy shivered. In the subterranean passage, cries for help would never be heard. She would be entirely at the mercy of anyone who found her trespassing.

Her own footsteps seemed strangely loud and echoed in her ears. Of, if only she would come to the end of the passage! Surely, it could not run on forever.

The air was cold and damp, and in a number of places water dripped from the ceiling. Nancy believed that it was rain dripping through the cracks in the cement. In that case she could not be far underground.

Where did the tunnel lead? Perhaps it came out in someone's garden or a wood.

"And maybe to a graveyard." Nancy shivered. "I've heard of such things. Anyway, I hope not. I've gone through enough for one night!"

Her head ached from the injury she had received, and she was tired from nervous strain. She was impatient to reach the end of the passage.

What would she find there? She could only hope that the exit would not be barred. If such were the case, she would be a prisoner in the underground vault. Of course she could always return to the entrance, but whether or not she could find the hidden spring which controlled the sliding panel was another matter.

After a time she stopped a moment to rest.

As she paused she heard a sound directly behind her. Wheeling, she suppressed a cry of terror.

A big rat scurried by, almost at her feet.

"Ug!" Nancy shuddered. "I don't like this place."

Still, she would not turn back. After resting a few minutes she again proceeded.

The passage was no longer straight, but twisted and turned in a puzzling fashion. At one place she came to a point where two tunnels branched off. She hesitated, uncertain, which one to take.

After a short mental debate she selected the right hand one, but as she went on, could not help but feel she had chosen the wrong one. Perhaps she was returning to Gombet's house, doubling back on her trail.

Anxiously, Nancy, glanced at her flashlight. She had forgotten to bring an extra battery and she did not know how long the present one would last. The bright light somewhat reassured her, but nevertheless she quickened her pace. She could think of nothing more horrifying than to be left without a light in such a gruesome place.

She tried to take note of the various turns in the tunnel but presently gave it up as a hopeless task. If she were forced to return, she must depend upon instinct to guide her.

"I hope I don't get lost," she worried. "That would be the crowning misfortune."

At last her foot struck a hard object, and Nancy quickly turned her flashlight upon it. She had reached another stone step. Perhaps she was approaching the exit to the passageway.

The thought gave her new courage. As she peered ahead she saw a long flight of stone steps leading upward. Eagerly, she groped her way up them.

It seemed to her that the air became gradually warmer and less damp.

"I'm coming out of the tunnel at last," she reasoned joyfully. "I wonder where I am?"

At last the stone steps came to an end, but to her chagrin, Nancy faced a solid wall.

"There must be a secret spring, if only I can find it," she thought desperately.

Anxiously, she flashed her light over the wall. Near the top step she saw a tiny knob not unlike the one she had discovered in the closet of Nathan Gombet's house. With a cry of satisfaction, she pushed upon it.

Slowly, the wall swung back, and in amazement Nancy passed through the opening. The panel grated shut behind her.

"This is positively spooky," she laughed uncertainly. "Who ever dreamed there was a place like this anywhere near Cliffwood? It reminds me of the feudal castles. The man who built it certainly had funny ideas."

If Nancy had expected to find herself at the mouth of the passage she was mistaken. Ahead of her was a steep flight of wooden stairs.

The steps were very old and offered treacherous footing, and the space between the walls was so narrow that it was with difficulty that she proceeded. She moved forward cautiously feeling each step.

She had climbed but a short distance when she stepped forward with her right foot and instead of striking a solid base, found nothing beneath. Only by grasping the step above did she save herself from a fall.

Quickly focusing the light down upon the step, she was able to see that the bottom of it was missing. The flooring had rotted entirely away.

"That was a lucky escape," she said inwardly. "I might have broken my leg there."

Carefully avoiding the hole, she moved on. A dozen more steps and she reached a landing. Here several narrow flights of stairs branched off. What could it mean? Where was she?

Nancy felt reasonably certain that that she was inside a house, but whether she had returned to Gombet's dwelling, she had no way of telling.

After a slight hesitation she selected one of

the flights and continued to climb. The steps were in terrible condition and at any moment she expected to crash through the half-decayed wood.

Far above, she thought she could see a dim light filtering through a crack, and she hurried eagerly on. She was so anxious to reach the top of the stairs that she failed to notice that her flashlight was growing dimmer and dimmer.

Just as she came to the end of the steps, the light blinked. Then for the first time Nancy glanced down and saw that the bulb was dim. The battery was nearly exhausted. A few moments more, and she would be plunged in darkness.

Ahead she caught a glimpse of a huge metal ring on the wall. What it was she had no idea, but it offered her her only hope of escape from the staircase.

Just as her hand reached out and grasped it, the flashlight flickered again. Then it went entirely out.

Nancy Drew was left in darkness.

CHAPTER XXI

The End of the Passage

Panic momentarily took possession of Nancy Drew as her light flickered out. She was a prisoner within the secret staircase. Without a light there was little hope that she could find the exit.

After her first fright had passed, she began to think more logically. Through a crack in the wall, a dim light filtered. Unquestionably, she had reached the end of the passage, and if only she could find the secret, the wall would open.

"Perhaps the metal ring will open the panel," she thought hopefully.

Grasping it firmly with both hands, she pulled with all her strength. A trapdoor fell back so unexpectedly that Nancy nearly lost her balance and tumbled down the stairs. Only by maintaining her hold on the ring did she save herself.

Beyond the opening she could see a room. Where was she? Had she doubled back and thus returned to Nathan Gombet's dwelling?

Scarcely daring to breath lest her presence be discovered, she crawled through the opening and hastily scrambled to her feet.

The room was dimly lighted by one window, and as she glanced toward it, Nancy was surprised to see the moonbeams shining upon the casement. Evidently, she had been within the passage for some time, as it had stopped raining.

In the dim light she could not make out her surroundings. She moved forward with the utmost caution. As she groped her way, she reached out with her hand and touched something. It was a piece of furniture. Eagerly, she felt of it, and then smiled broadly.

She knew that old highboy. She remembered seeing it the day she had searched the Turnbull attic!

Nancy's anxiety fell from her like a cloak. She leaned against the highboy and chuckled softly. Now she knew where she was!

She had traveled from Gombet's house underground to the Turnbull mansion. The stairs she had ascended had led up the side of the house to the attic. Undoubtedly, the other flights she had passed led to other portions of the old house.

But why had she failed to discover the trapdoor when she had first examined the attic, she asked herself. Certainly, she had made a thorough search.

"I can't see a thing without a light," she grumbled mentally. "I suppose I'll have to wait until morning before I can investigate this attic again."

Nancy did not close the trapdoor, for she was afraid that if she did she might never again find the spring which opened it. In the morning she would visit the attic and again enter the hidden staircase.

"Now I'll go to my room and try to sleep," she decided. "It's long past midnight and I'm dead tired."

Softly, she crept forward, feeling her way out of the attic. She found the stairs which led to the floor below, and quietly descended them.

"I hope Floretta and Rosemary don't hear me," she chuckled. "If they do they'll think the ghost is abroad again."

She slipped past Rosemary's bedroom and reached her own in safety.

"What an adventure!" she sighed happily, as she closed the bedroom door behind her and lighted a candle. "What a night! I hope I'll never go through another as harrowing. Still, I wouldn't have missed it for worlds!"

Hastily, she undressed and crawled into bed,

but she did not fall to sleep at once. Instead, she lay awake staring up at the ceiling.

As she pieced together the information she had secured from every source, she comprehended the value of her night's work. She understood it all now. Nathan Gombet was the guilty party. It was he who had visited the Turnbull mansion at frequent intervals, frightening the old ladies and stealing their valuables.

Since Nancy had learned that he wished to buy the Turnbull property at a ridiculously low figure, she had been convinced that it was Nathan who made nightly visits to the mansion, but without definite proof of her theory she could not lay her case before the authorities. Now she had the necessary proof!

Probably the secret tunnel which connected Gombet's house with the Turnbull residence had been built before Civil War days, and had been planned as a protection against possible marauders. At that time the Turnbull brothers had been friendly and Nancy imagined that they used the passage frequently as a means of going from one house to the other. But with the Civil War, the brothers had become enemies, and the passageway had been closed up. With the passing of the years it had been forgotten, until now the descendants could recall nothing about it.

In some way, undoubtedly by accident, Nathan Gombet had stumbled upon the entrance. He had determined to use the knowledge to further his own ugly schemes.

"Probably there are openings on each floor," Nancy thought. "It would be easy for Nathan to go from one room to another without being discovered, it would be just like him to hide and listen to any conversation he could!"

She recalled the strange threatening note she had received which had warned her not to meddle with the affairs of the Trumbulls. She was convinced that Gombet had sent the message. He had heard Floretta and Rosemary discussing the letter, and in that way had learned that she was expected to arrive.

The loss of the pocketbook, the silver spoon, the urn, the pin, and Floretta's dresses could be easily explained. Nathan had entered the house by the secret staircase and had taken the things.

"There must be an opening into the library," Nancy told herself. "I intend to find it tomorrow if I have to chop down the wall!"

It was no longer a mystery how the canaries had reached Floretta's room. Probably Nathan had accidentally left the entrance to the tunnel open on one of his visits to the mansion, and the birds had flown through the opening and had found their way to the house, or possibly the miser had brought them with him.

The loud cry which had been heard in the night was easily explained. Nathan Gombet had fallen over the broken step on the stairway and had hurt himself.

"Served him right, too," Nancy thought, with some pleasure.

Satisfied that she had solved the mystery, she turned over in bed and tried to go to sleep. But she could not. Worries began to beset her.

Until Nathan Gombet was brought to justice her work was not accomplished. It would not be easy to capture him, she knew, for the miser was a desperate man when crossed. If only her father were at home to give her advice!

"What can have become of him?" she fretted, as she tossed restlessly in bed. "I'm so worried. If I don't hear from him to-morrow I must report him missing to the police!"

Not until it was nearly dawn did she fall into a troubled sleep.

CHAPTER XXII

The Next Move

When Nancy Drew opened her eyes the following morning, the sun was streaming in at her bedroom window. A quick glance at the clock on her dresser disclosed that it was fifteen minutes past nine.

"Horrors!" she cried, springing from the bed. "Why didn't Floretta or Rosemary awaken me?"

She was provoked with herself that she had overslept on a morning when she had so much to do. Although she had gone through a trying ordeal the night before, she was none the worse for the experience, and arose feeling refreshed and eager for what the day might bring forth.

Hastily dressing, she hurried downstairs to find that breakfast was waiting.

"You have no idea how sorry I am," she apologized contritely. "You shouldn't have waited for me."

"It doesn't matter in the least," Rosemary

told her quietly, as the three sat down to the breakfast table. "This may be the last breakfast we'll ever eat here."

"Why, what do you mean?" Nancy glanced up quickly and noticed the sad expression on the faces of the Turnbull sisters.

"Nathan Gombet was here this morning," Rosemary explained.

Nancy's spoon clattered from her hand.

"He was here this morning?" she asked in astonishment.

"Yes, he came to repeat the offer he made us some time ago for the house."

"That wasn't an offer—it was a steal!"

"But in the light of what has happened here, we can't expect to get much for the house."

"You didn't sell?" Nancy questioned anxiously.

"We have made up our minds to give up the house. Yes, we accepted his offer and told him that if he came back this afternoon we would sign the papers."

"Then you haven't signed anything yet?"

"Not yet," Rosemary responded listlessly.

"Oh, I'm so glad!" Nancy cried impulsively. "If you had it would have spoiled everything. There is no need for you ever to leave your home," she added impressively. "You see, I've solved the mystery at last."

"You've solved the mystery?" Floretta demanded eagerly. "You know what became of our silver urn? Oh, it's too good to be true!"

"I can't lay hands on your urn this minute," Nancy told her. "But I think I can get it within twenty-four hours."

"Don't keep us in suspense," Rosemary begged. "Tell us everything. Is there really a ghost in our house?"

Nancy laughed.

"Nathan Gombet is the ghost—just as I suspected."

"Are you certain?" Rosemary asked a trifle doubtfully. "He has been our neighbor for years and he offered to buy our house."

"That's just why he has been trying to frighten you. Because he wanted to force you to sell at his price."

"I always thought Nathan was mean, but I had no idea he would do a thing like that," Floretta said. "Have you really the proof that he is the guilty party? Unless you have, we wouldn't dare accuse him."

"I'll show you my proof," Nancy declared. "Come with me and I think you'll be convinced."

Hurrying to the kitchen, she secured a supply of candles, and then led the way to the attic. Wonderingly, Rosemary and Floretta followed.

Nancy flung open the door and permitted the Turnbull sisters to enter first.

"I have discovered a hidden stairway," she informed them, as she flashed her candle in the direction of the old highboy.

Rosemary and Floretta took one look and gasped in astonishment. The secret stairway was plainly revealed for the trapdoor was open just as Nancy had left it the night before.

"Who ever dreamed of a hidden staircase in our house?" Floretta demanded in excitement.

"There were rumors to that effect," Rosemary admitted. "But I never believed them. Just think how many times we've been in this attic and never discovered the trapdoor!"

"It was very cleverly hidden," Nancy told them. "I searched and couldn't find it myself from the outside."

"Where does the stairway lead?" Floretta asked, peering into the dark recess.

"It leads to a tunnel which connects The Mansion with Nathan Gombet's house."

"And he's been entering our house nightly by means of this staircase?" Floretta questioned.

"I'm convinced of it."

"But how did you ever make the discovery?" Rosemary broke in admiringly.

Nancy then told the details of her harrowing experience in the Gombet residence. She ended by showing them the bump on her head which had been caused by falling down the stone steps.

"You might have been killed," Floretta shuddered. "And imagine going through that passage all alone in the dead of night! It must have been terrible! I never could have done it."

"I'll admit I didn't enjoy the experience," Nancy replied. "But it was the only way to solve the mystery."

Rosemary, who had been studying the entrance to the staircase meditatively, now turned to Nancy with a puzzled frown.

"There's one thing that isn't clear to me. I don't see how Nathan took our silver urn from the library and managed to escape without being caught. In order to reach this staircase it would be necessary for him to pass our bedrooms. Surely, we would have heard him."

"That puzzles me too," Nancy admitted. "But I have a theory which I intend to investigate this morning. I believe there must be another opening to this staircase on the floor below."

"Perhaps there's one in every room," Floretta speculated.

"It wouldn't surprise me to find one on every floor," Nancy stated.

"But we searched thoroughly," Rosemary protested. "We went over every inch of the walls."

"That's true. But I believe it will be easier to find the openings from the inside. I intend to enter the staircase again and try to find them. Last night I remember that several flight of stairs branched off from one landing. I want to find out where they lead. Do you want to go with me?"

"Certainly," Rosemary declared promptly. "I have a great curiosity to see what the stairway is like."

"It's so old we must be careful not to fall," Nancy warned her. "One of the steps has rotted away entirely."

As she spoke, she stepped through the opening into the passageway. Rosemary boldly followed, but Floretta hesitated uncertainly.

"What if the trapdoor should fall shut?" she questioned anxiously.

"I'm sure it won't," Nancy reassured her. "But even if it does, I can open it again. See, here is the hidden spring."

She held her candle so that the beam illuminated the metal ring which controlled the door. Still, Floretta hesitated.

"Do hurry," Rosemary commanded impatiently. "There's no danger."

Floretta folded her skirts tightly about her to prevent them from brushing against the dusty walls, and then timidly descended the first step.

"I don't like it," she choked. "The dust is terrific and the cobwebs—ug!" Nevertheless, she did not turn back.

Cautiously, Nancy Drew led the way down the wooden stairs, taking care to avoid the broken step. At the landing she selected one of the passages which led in another direction, and descended the stairs until she came to another landing.

As she flashed her light about, her keen eyes caught the gleam of a metal ring. She seized upon it eagerly.

"This must open a panel," she cried, in excitement.

As she pulled upon the ring, the wall fell away, and to her amazement she stepped into a closet which was filled with garments.

"Where are we?" she demanded.

"Why, we must be in my room!" Floretta gasped. "Now I understand what became of my silk dresses and the diamond pin!"

"It's clear Nathan must have entered the room by means of the secret panel in the closet," Rosemary observed.

"But how did the canaries get in?" Floretta demanded.

"They might have flown through the passage and entered the room when the panel was open," Nancy suggested.

"That's very likely," Rosemary agreed. "It's no wonder we thought the walls had ears. It's my opinion Nathan has been hiding in the staircase listening to everything we say. It frightens me to think of it!"

"I feel confident it was Nathan Gombet who sent me the threatening letter advising me not to come to this house," Nancy declared. "Can you remember whether or not you read my letter aloud after it arrived?"

"Yes, we did," Floretta responded quickly. "And we were in this very bedroom too! Nathan must have been listening and heard every word!"

"It's clear enough now," Rosemary said caustically. "That man thought he could frighten us from our home. To think we nearly sold The Mansion to him!"

"Shall we investigate the other passages?" Nancy questioned. "Our time is getting short and I'm eager to find out where they lead."

"By all means," Rosemary agreed.

Without taking time to close the panel after them, the three descended the hidden stairway to the landing below and there selected another flight of wooden stairs.

"We must be going down to the first floor now," Floretta observed, as they cautiously descended.

"Watch out for the step," Nancy, who was ahead, called out in warning. "There's another broken one just ahead."

The three avoided the hole in the flooring and continued down the staircase. At last, Nancy came to the end of the passage, but to her surprise could find no hidden panel. In vain she flashed her candle about over the walls and Floretta and Rosemary aided in the search.

"That's funny," Nancy murmured in perplexity. "I'm sure there must be an opening here somewhere."

She glanced anxiously at her candle. It would not last many more minutes, and unless she wished to be plunged into darkness, she must return to the kitchen for another supply. Floretta and Rosemary had used the last of their stock.

The passage at this particular place was very narrow and so low that a person could not stand upright without striking the top wall.

Tiring of the stooped position which she had been forced to endure for several minutes, Nancy straightened. Her head struck the top of the passageway.

"Ouch!" she exclaimed.

To her astonishment, she heard a strange clicking noise.

"I believe I've discovered the panel," she cried eagerly.

While Rosemary held the candle, she examined ceiling overhead and pushed upon it with all her strength. To her surprise, the wall gave way easily and lifted up.

Nancy pushed the obstruction out of the way and thrust her head and shoulders through the opening. Curiously, she gazed about. She had come up through the sofa seat in the library!

"My word!" she exclaimed. "No wonder I never found the secret panel in this room. Who would have thought of looking in the sofa!"

She pulled herself up through the opening and then assisted Floretta and Rosemary, who were less athletic.

"Mercy! What next?" Floretta gasped as she sank down into a chair and tried to regain her breath.

"Imagine living in this house all these years and never discovering anything wrong with that sofa!" Rosemary commented.

"I see everything now," Nancy said slowly. "That broken step just before we came to the opening. Nathan must have fallen and cried out in alarm. And I feel certain there must be another opening in the sofa in the drawing room. I'm going to find out!"

Darting into the next room, she jerked the cushions from the sofa and lifted the base boards. As she had suspected, there was an opening similar to the one in the library, which was just large enough for a person to squeeze through.

"That's how Nathan stole the silver urn," Floretta observed. "He came up through the sofa seat in the library!"

"How stupid of me not to think of looking there before," Nancy said.

"Stupid? I think you've done extremely clever detective work, as it is. Why, we've lived here for years and never dreamed of a hidden staircase. How shall we ever repay you for all you have done?"

"Oh, let's not think about that now," Nancy said hastily, glancing at her watch. "There's so much yet to be done. We must bring Nathan Gombet to justice if we can!"

"I agree with you there," Floretta cried feelingly. "Go and call the police! We want him locked up!"

Nancy started toward the door.

"If he has an inkling of what we have discovered, he'll try to escape," she threw back over her shoulder.

She hurried to the garage at the rear of the

house and quickly backed her roadster out upon the drive. Rosemary and Floretta, not to be left behind, crowded in beside her.

"Oh, do you think the police will be able to capture him?" Floretta asked tremulously. "I'll never feel safe again until I know he's behind prison bars."

"I'm afraid we shouldn't have taken the time we did to investigate those passages," Nancy returned quietly. "But I wanted to be absolutely certain that Nathan Gombet was guilty before I turned him over to the authorities."

With that she shifted gears, and the car roared down the Cliffwood road to disappear in a cloud of dust.

CHAPTER XXIII

Notifying the Police

"Oh, if only we had installed a telephone at the mansion," Rosemary fretted, as Nancy Drew's roadster sped along over the smooth road toward Cliffwood.

"Isn't there any house along the road where we can stop to call the police?" Nancy questioned. "It would save us considerable time."

Rosemary shook her head.

"There aren't any houses until we get almost into Cliffwood."

"Then we may as well drive straight to the sheriff's office," Nancy decided. "It's only a short distance, anyway. A few minutes delay ought not to make such a big difference."

"But it may," Floretta declared uneasily. "I believe Nathan is beginning to be suspicious. Otherwise, he wouldn't have come to us this morning with the offer to buy the house."

Nancy did not respond, but concentrated her attention upon the road before her. In exactly twelve minutes flat she brought the automobile to a quivering halt in front of the sheriff's office.

Switching off the engine, she sprang from the car, and, with the Turnbull sisters close behind her, ran into the building. The sheriff, the picture of repose, with his feet comfortably placed on the top of a roll-top desk, was laughing and talking with several men who were seated about the room. As Nancy Drew and the two women came in, he swung his feet to the floor and eyed them with respectful attention.

"Anything I can do for you?" he inquired.

Without mincing words, Nancy quickly told of the strange things that had happened at the Turnbull house and of the discoveries she had made. At various points, Rosemary and Floretta corroborated her story.

"I want you to arrest Nathan Gombet," Nancy ended. "He is the guilty man."

The sheriff scratched his head in perplexity.

"Well, I don't know what to say. Nathan Gombet is no friend of mine and folks say he's a little queer, but I never heard of his doing any harm."

"There's always a first time," Rosemary snapped.

"He's just a clever crook—that's all," Nancy declared impatiently. "Don't you believe our story? We can show you the staircase."

"Yes, I believe your story, all right," the sheriff said hastily. "But I dasn't proceed without evidence. You can't arrest a man unless you've some proof he's guilty."

"What more proof do you want?" Rosemary interposed tartly.

"Well, if you'd found the silver urn in his house, or something like that——"

"If my father were here, he'd convince you all right," Nancy said, with rising temper.

"Your father?"

"Yes, Carson Drew."

"You don't mean Carson Drew, the lawyer from River Heights? You're his daughter?"

"I am."

"Well, that's different. Why didn't you say so at first?"

"What has that to do with the case?"

"Well, I reckon a daughter of Carson Drew knows what she's about. If you say Nathan Gombet is a crook, I'll take your word for it."

"Well, it seems to me you've taken plenty of time to make up your mind," Nancy said sarcastically.

The sheriff, thus goaded to action, turned to the other men in the room. His indolent manner fell from him.

"Come on, boys!" he shouted.

Turning to Nancy he ordered:

"You lead the way and we'll follow."

Nancy nodded, and with Floretta and Rosemary hurried outside to the waiting roadster.

"I never could stand that sheriff," Rosemary commented. "You can see now why we didn't like to put the matter in his hands before. He would have made a mess of it."

"I can see all right," Nancy admitted dryly.

She sprang into the car and the Turnbull sisters climbed in beside her. She started the motor and waited impatiently for the sheriff and his deputies. The moment the police car was ready to leave, she shifted gears and was off.

As the two cars raced down the side streets of Cliffwood, many passersby turned to stare curiously after them. Nancy did not notice, for she was intent only upon one thing, and that was to reach the old stone house before Nathan Gombet had an opportunity to escape or to hide the booty he had stolen from the Turnbull mansion.

"The sheriff may be stupid enough to refuse to arrest him unless he finds *evidence* on the place," she thought, in disgust.

She drove swiftly and soon came within sight of the gloomy old stone house owned by the miser. Believing that it would be wisest to approach cautiously and not give an alarm, she slowed down. To her chagrin the police car raced ahead and roared down the driveway. It came to a sudden halt in front of the house.

The sheriff sprang from the automobile and turned to his men.

"Surround the house!" he ordered crisply. "We won't take any chance on letting that old boy get away!"

"Oh, why does that sheriff have to be so dramatic?" Nancy murmured, in alarm. "After all this noise, it will be a wonder if Nathan Gombet doesn't slip through the secret tunnel and escape. That will ruin everything!"

Impatiently, she opened the door of the roadster and started to get out, but Floretta held her back.

"Don't go," she begged. "There may be shooting!"

Nancy permitted herself to be pulled back into the safety of the automobile. From there, the three watched the sheriff with misgiving. They saw him walk up to the back door and knock. When there was no response, he knocked again. He tried the door, but it was locked. Then he peeped in at the kitchen window.

"No one at home," he muttered in disgust, turning away.

Nancy could stand it no longer. Springing

from the roadster, she ran toward the sheriff.

"You can't expect Nathan Gombet to welcome you with open arms after all the noise you made coming up the drive," she cried. "He'd be more apt to welcome you with buckshot! He's probably watching now from an upstairs window. We'd all make good targets!"

The sheriff glanced anxiously upward and stepped closer to the house.

"It's pretty serious business to go breaking into a man's house," he said, somewhat crestfallen, "unless you're mighty sure you've got the right man."

"Nathan Gombet is the right man!"

"Well, maybe he is, I don't know." The sheriff's old doubt was returning to assail him anew. "I suppose I could ram the door, but I don't like to do it."

"I'll assume the responsibility," Nancy said shortly.

"All right, we'll do it."

"There's an easier way."

"How do you mean?"

"Climb through the cellar window and get in that way. There's a stairway from the cellar leading to the kitchen."

"That's an idea."

The sheriff motioned to his deputies, and Nancy led the way to the cellar window. One by one the men crawled in. Nancy hesitated an instant, and then she followed.

Silently, she indicated the stairs leading to the kitchen. The sheriff and his deputies crept quietly up to the landing, and there they paused and listened. The house was as silent as a tomb.

Then unmistakably, there was a slight shuffling sound which seemed to come from the kitchen. The sheriff turned to a deputy near him and whispered into his ear:

"Did you hear that?"

"Yes, chief," the deputy whispered in reply. "There's someone hiding in that kitchen!"

"Get set, boys, we'll see who it is!"

The sheriff placed his hand on the door knob and gave it a quick turn. The latch clicked. As the sheriff thrust open the door, he started back involuntarily, for he stood looking straight into the muzzle of a sawed off shotgun, held in the hands of Gombet's colored servant!

CHAPTER XXIV

NANCY LEADS THE WAY

THE old colored woman advanced threateningly, her face convulsed with rage.

"You git, white man!" she ordered, "or I'll fill yo' system full of lead."

Somewhat sheepishly, the sheriff retreated. He dared not reach for his own revolver which hung in its holster, lest the colored woman carry out her threat. As he backed away, the negress slammed the door and locked it.

"I reckon we'll have to take the place by storm," the sheriff muttered to his companions. "She's locked the door. We'll have to ram it."

"And while we're doing it, she'll pepper us with shot," one of the deputies observed.

"I reckon you're right, at that," the sheriff said slowly. "I guess we'd better fire a volley through the door."

"We haven't any call to kill the woman," a deputy argued. "And a stray shot might hit her. We don't want to do that."

"That's so. Anyone have an idea how we can get into the house?"

"I have," Nancy Drew announced quickly. "I know of a secret passage which leads from the Turnbull mansion to an upstairs room of this house. Give me two men, and the rest stay here to keep watch. We'll get into the house through the passage and take her by surprise."

"That's an idea," the sheriff murmured. "I'll go with you myself." He indicated one of the deputies. "You come along too. The rest of you boys stay here."

"And make a little racket every so often to hold the attention of the old colored woman," Nancy suggested.

"When we get into the kitchen I'll blow my police whistle," the sheriff added. "When you hear it, rush up from below."

The sheriff and the deputy assigned to the venture, followed Nancy Drew from the cellar. They crept past the kitchen window and hurried toward the police car. There was no time for Nancy to stop to explain matters to Rosemary and Floretta. They sat huddled in the roadster where she had left them a few minutes before.

"They'll be safe enough so long as they stay in the car," the sheriff said, as the three ran across the courtyard and sprang into the po-

ing the stone steps, she groped about the walls, searching for the hidden spring which would open the panel.

"Look for a brass ring or a tiny knob," she directed the two men.

Even as she whispered the instruction, her hand struck a solid object on the wall. Eagerly, she felt of it and discovered it was a small metal ring.

"I've found it!" she whispered in delight.

She gave the ring a hard pull, and, to the amazement of the sheriff and his deputy, the secret panel opened.

Nancy stepped out into the light and motioned for the two men to follow. She now stood in the closet of the bird room. Cautiously opening the closet door, she peered out.

"The coast is clear," she informed her companions quietly. "Follow me."

Softly, she tiptoed across the room and tried the door leading into the corridor. It was unlocked. Treading quietly down the hall, she led the way to the stairs.

Reaching the lower floor, Nancy Drew and the officers crept toward the kitchen where the belligerent old colored servant had taken up her post.

The sheriff listened for a moment at the inner door of the kitchen and peered through the keyhole. The old woman had not relinquished the gun, but stood before the basement door making vehement threats.

"I's waitin' fo' you," she muttered. "You just make one pass t'rough dat doah and I's gwine lose control o' mah trigger finger. I'll fill you so full o' buckshot dat you'll look like a sieve, and I don't mean possibly."

Satisfied that the old negress was occupied at the basement door, the sheriff quickly stepped into the room and covered her with his pistol.

"You're under arrest!" he said sharply.

The colored woman turned suddenly and gazed into the muzzle of the sheriff's gun. She hesitated an instant as if debating whether it would be wise to attempt resistance, then threw up her hands in surrender. The shotgun clattered to the floor.

Nancy Drew, who by this time had rushed into the room, ran to the basement door and unlocked it. As the sheriff gave one short blast on his police whistle, the deputies who had been left stationed below burst into the kitchen. One of them caught up the shotgun from the floor and placed it out of reach. Another quickly slipped handcuffs on the woman's wrists.

"Now that we have her, what are we going to do with her?" the sheriff asked bluntly.

Nancy turned toward him.

"Sheriff, may I question the prisoner?"

"Go ahead; but I'm afraid you'll not get much out of her."

"I'll try, anyway," Nancy said, smiling. She faced the negress and demanded:

"Where is Nathan Gombet?"

"How come you asks me? I ain't keepin' track o' dat man just 'cause I works heah."

"You're not fooling anyone," Nancy replied sharply. "I know that you are not only Nathan Gombet's servant but his partner in crime as well."

The woman assumed an innocent expression.

"How you talk! Crime? What you mean crime? I's just an old culled woman who makes her victuals workin'! You can't bluff me with yo' scary talk."

"I'm not bluffing. It will be the best for you to tell us where he is. If you don't, you'll be behind bars within an hour."

"Fo' doin' what?"

"For resisting an officer. Isn't that true, sheriff?"

"Yes, I reckon it is," the sheriff returned. "The woman has laid herself open to imprisonment by trying to thwart justice."

"Now will you tell?" Nancy looked straight into the old negress' eyes as she asked the question.

For a moment the woman met her gaze defiantly and then a frightened look came over her face and she began to whine.

"I'll tell! I'll tell! Don't send me to no jail!" she implored. "Please, Mr. Sheriff!"

"Then, if you don't want to go to jail, tell us where Nathan Gombet is hiding."

The colored woman eyed the girl sullenly for an instant, and then pointed to the floor above.

"Up dar!" she mumbled. "He's up dar with de prisoner."

"Prisoner!" Nancy exclaimed, giving the sheriff a quick glance. "What prisoner?"

The colored woman stubbornly shook her head.

"We'll find out who you mean," Nancy declared. She turned to the sheriff with decision. "We must capture Nathan Gombet before he escapes. If he's upstairs he may have heard us and try to get away through the secret passage!"

"He'll not get away," the sheriff assured her grimly.

Delegating one man to remain below to guard the colored woman, he ordered the other deputies to follow him. Nancy, who could not bear to remain behind, crept up the stairs after them.

At the top landing the party paused, undecided which way to go. As they hesitated, the sound of a harsh, rasping voice reached their ears.

"Listen!" Nancy commanded in a tense whisper.

Instantly, she recognized the voice. It belonged to Nathan Gombet!

As she listened intently, the man began to speak again and she caught the words distinctly.

"I give you just one minute, Carson Drew! If you don't sign that paper before then I'll——"

Nancy did not hear the rest of the threat, for Nathan's voice had dropped to a lower pitch. What could it mean? Had Nathan held her father a prisoner in the house? She turned frightened eyes toward the sheriff.

"They're in that room," she whispered, pointing to the chamber in which her father was imprisoned.

The sheriff nodded, and with his pistol held ready for instant use, moved softly toward the room. Quick as he was, Nancy was ahead of him.

Without a thought for her own safety, now that she knew her father was in danger, she flung open the door.

At a glance she took in the situation. Her father, haggard and pale with suffering, was bound to a chair and Nathan Gombet, a taunting grin on his evil face, was bending over him.

"If you don't sign this paper, you'll never get out of here!" he snarled.

At the sound of the opening door, the miser wheeled about and saw Nancy Drew. As he instinctively retreated, she advanced.

"The police will have something to say to you!" she said tensely.

As Nancy Drew spoke, the sheriff and his men closed in around Nathan Gombet.

"Your game's up," the sheriff announced, covering the miser with his pistol.

CHAPTER XXV

Captured

Nathan Gombet's shifty eyes roved to the door, and, suddenly, he made a spring for it. One of the deputies caught him roughly by the arm and dragged him back.

"Oh, no, you don't!"

"Handcuff him," the sheriff ordered.

The miser saw that escape was cut off entirely. As the realization came over him, he wilted and offered little resistance when the handcuffs were snapped upon his wrists.

Nancy immediately lost interest in the miser and ran to her father. Frantically she began to work at the ropes which bound him to the chair.

"Oh, Dad!" she murmured brokenly, "are you hurt?"

"I'll be all right," Carson Drew forced a wan smile. "Couldn't have stood it much longer, though. If you hadn't come just when you did——"

With the aid of one of the deputies who had

a knife, Nancy quickly cut the ropes and set her father free. In relief he stretched his cramped limbs.

Slowly getting upon his feet, he took a step forward and would have collapsed had Nancy not helped him. Wearily, he sank down upon the chair again.

"Legs feel paralyzed," he complained.

"Don't you want me to call a doctor?" Nancy asked, as she began to rub the cramped muscles.

Carson Drew shook his head.

"No, I'll be all right after a while. I'm just weak. If only I could have a glass of water! That fiend hasn't given me anything to eat or drink for more than twenty-four hours. My throat is parched."

"I'll get you a drink!" Nancy cried.

She darted from the room and hurried downstairs to the kitchen. Pumping a cold drink of water at the sink, she paused only long enough to step to the outside door and call Rosemary and Floretta Turnbull, who were still waiting anxiously in the roadster. They came in response to her summons, and followed her upstairs.

"Tell us everything, Dad," Nancy begged, as she gave her father the glass of water.

Carson Drew set down the tumbler which he

had emptied at one draught and fastened his eyes upon Nathan Gombet.

"That man induced me to come here by trickery," he explained, a hard glint coming into his eyes. "He has tortured me here for several days trying to force me to sign over money to him."

"Well, he won't try any more of his tricks," the sheriff broke in. "We'll have him behind prison bars inside of twenty minutes." He turned to the prisoner. "What have you to say for yourself?"

"Nothing," Gombet muttered sullenly.

"Do you admit that you were trying to get money which did not belong to you?" Carson Drew questioned sharply.

Nathan Gombet did not reply.

"You'll talk all right when we get you to the station," the sheriff told him harshly. "It's no use to deny your guilt. You were caught in the act." He picked up a piece of paper from the table and glanced at it. "Is this the agreement he was trying to force you to sign, Mr. Drew?"

The lawyer nodded.

"Yes, he wanted me to turn over a large sum of money and then promise not to prosecute."

The sheriff folded the paper and put it in his pocket.

"I'll just keep this for evidence."

"And don't forget, he tried to force us from our home," Rosemary Turnbull broke in. "We intend to file a charge against him."

"I didn't mean no harm," Gombet grunted.

"Oh, no," Rosemary retorted sarcastically. "I suppose those nightly visits of yours were merely friendly calls."

"I thought I saw an easy way to make a little money. I offered to buy your house."

"Yes—at your price," Floretta sniffed.

"It was a cowardly trick—to try to cheat two women," Carson Drew observed.

"He nearly succeeded, too," Rosemary declared feelingly. "If it hadn't been for Nancy Drew, we would have been forced to give up our home. We couldn't have stood it there another day."

For some time Nancy had remained silent, but now she turned to the old miser.

"When did you first discover the hidden staircase?" she questioned curiously.

Nathan hesitated as though debating whether or not to tell.

"You'd better make a clean breast of everything. It will go easier with you if you do," the sheriff warned him.

"It was two months ago," Nathan muttered. "Found the hidden spring by accident."

"You explored the staircase and discovered that it led to the Turnbull mansion?"

Gombet nodded.

"How many openings are there into this house?"

"Only the one in the room where I keep my birds."

"There's one more thing I want to know," Nancy continued. "It was you who sent me the threatening note, warning me not to come to the Turnbull mansion, wasn't it?"

"Yes, I sent it," the man grunted.

"How did you learn that I was going there?"

"Hid in the staircase and heard the old ladies talking about the letter you'd sent."

"Just as I suspected. And now where are the things you took from their house?"

"What things?"

"Oh, you needn't pretend," Floretta broke in, enraged. "You took our silver urn and a diamond pin."

"And a pocketbook and a silver spoon, to say nothing of Floretta's silk dresses," Rosemary added severely.

"I don't know what you're talking about."

"Oh, yes you do," Nancy told him quietly. "It won't do you any good to deny it, for we intend to search the house from cellar to garret. You may as well tell us what you have done with the things."

Nathan Gombet debated the question silently and then muttered reluctantly:

"You'll find 'em in my room."

"Which room is that?"

"Straight across the hall."

Nancy hurried from the room without waiting for more. Rosemary and Floretta followed her eagerly. As they flung open the door of the bedroom they gave a little cry of pleasure, for on the dresser stood the silver urn.

"What a relief!" Rosemary cried, rushing forward and snatching it up. "It's a wonder he didn't try to dispose of it."

Floretta, who had been investigating the closet, triumphantly brought out an armload of dresses.

"But where is the diamond pin?" Rosemary demanded. "That is the most valuable of all."

"Is this it?" Nancy, who had opened a bureau drawer, held up a tiny object.

Eagerly, Floretta reached for it.

"That's it. Oh, I'm so glad."

"And here is the spoon," Nancy continued, removing it from the drawer. "And the pocketbook. The money is gone though."

"Oh, we don't care about that," Rosemary said quickly. "There wasn't much in the pocketbook, anyway."

"Then everything is here," Nancy declared.

Armed with the booty, the three returned to

the chamber across the hall and disclosed their findings.

"It's a clear case of theft, all right," the sheriff said, as he examined the articles. "We'll take this fellow to jail and lock him up. He's a dangerous character and ought not to be at large."

"How about the negress?" Nancy questioned.

"She is an accomplice," Mr. Drew put in. "Take her along."

The sheriff grasped Nathan Gombet roughly by the arm and shoved him toward the door. Two of the deputies helped Carson Drew downstairs.

The old miser and the negress were put into the police car, and the sheriff and his men drove away, leaving Nancy and her father to say good-bye to the Turnbull sisters.

"We'll see to it that the various openings into the staircase are boarded up," Rosemary told the lawyer. "With Nathan in jail, we probably will never be bothered again." She regarded Carson Drew anxiously. "You don't look a bit well. You're in no condition to return to River Heights to-night."

"I think I can make it," Carson Drew replied.

"Nonsense. You must spend the night at The Mansion. Floretta and I will be delighted to have you. A good rest will do wonders for you. You need a good meal, too."

"To tell the truth, I don't feel very strong," the lawyer admitted. "Are you certain it won't inconvenience you if I stay?"

"Of course not. What a thing to ask, after all your daughter has done for us! No, it's all settled. You must stay at The Mansion until you have recovered your strength."

"And we'll promise you there will be no ghosts to trouble you," Floretta added, with a laugh.

So it was decided. Nancy helped her father into the roadster and drove him to The Mansion. As soon as she saw that he was comfortably settled on the sofa, she returned for the Turnbull sisters.

Although Carson Drew had suffered a great deal at the hands of Nathan Gombet, he had received no permanent injury. His strength gradually returned and he began to walk with less difficulty. Food and rest accomplished wonders. After a good night's rest he appeared at the breakfast table and announced that he felt able to travel.

"Oh, we were hoping you would stay another day," Floretta said regretfully, after the lawyer had announced his decision to return to River Heights that morning.

"I'm afraid I must go," the lawyer returned. "My business has been neglected the past week, you know. By the way, have you heard anything more about Nathan Gombet?"

"The entire story is in the morning papers," Rosemary turned to Nancy with a warm smile. "Haven't you seen them?"

"Not yet," Nancy admitted.

"You're certainly in the limelight," Floretta told her. "Evidently the reporters learned everything from the sheriff."

Nancy caught up one of the papers, and as her eye scanned the story on the front page a deep flush crept into her cheeks.

"Mercy! I don't deserve all the credit!" she protested modestly.

"Indeed, you do," Rosemary told her firmly. She glanced significantly at Floretta, who nodded firmly. "I hardly know how to begin," she went on, addressing Nancy with some hesitation. "But I want you to know how much Floretta and I appreciate what you have done for us."

"I was glad to do what little I could," Nancy declared graciously. "It was really fun for me. I thoroughly enjoy a mystery—though for a time I thought this one would prove my undoing."

"We want to reward you for what you did," Rosemary went on earnestly.

"Oh, I don't want any reward!" Nancy exclaimed. "You know, we discussed that before."

"We were afraid you wouldn't take money," Floretta sighed.

"So we've decided to give you a little gift as a remembrance," Rosemary continued. "We want you to accept our silver urn."

"Your urn!" Nancy gasped. "Oh, I couldn't do that! Why, it's a valuable heirloom and you prize it highly!"

"We want you to have it," Floretta insisted stubbornly. "We'll feel hurt if you don't take it."

"It will serve as a reminder of your adventure in The Mansion," Rosemary coaxed. "Please take it."

As she spoke she picked up a wrapped package from a table and handed it to Nancy.

"If you insist, I'm afraid I can't refuse," Nancy said, as she accepted the urn. "There's nothing in the world I'd rather have! This will make my second trophy! I'll keep it on the mantel with the clock!"

After thanking the Turnbull sisters for the gift and for their generous hospitality, Nancy and her father departed. Floretta and Rosemary watched them until they had disappeared down the road.

For a time Nancy and her father rode in silence, and then Carson Drew turned to his daughter with a look of deep admiration in his eyes.

"That was a neat piece of detective work you did," he said.

"Everything turned out all right," Nancy admitted. "But when I was going through that dark tunnel the night I discovered it, I told myself I'd never dabble in another mystery as long as I lived if I ever got out of there alive!"

"Do you intend to live up to that?"

"Not if I can help it! Now that you are safe and the mystery is solved, I'm aching for another one. I suppose that's all the good it will do be, though!"

"Oh, I don't know," Mr. Drew smiled. "This affair has won you quite a reputation."

Indeed, Nancy Drew's days of adventure were by no means over. Before many months had elapsed she was destined to be involved in another mystery case, equally as baffling as the one she had just solved. Readers who wish to follow her strange adventures may do so in the next volume of this series, entitled "The Bungalow Mystery."

But as Nancy Drew drove along the smooth road she had no idea of what was in store for her, and so it was that a semi-melancholy expression settled over her face. Carson Drew, who noticed the look, laughed aloud.

"You're a true daughter of your old dad all right, Nancy! Pining for another mystery before you're well out of this one!"

"Oh, I wasn't pining exactly," Nancy declared gayly, resolutely shaking off the mood of despondency which had claimed her for the moment. "I just couldn't help thinking that perhaps this would be my last chance to solve a mystery. And I do enjoy detective work!"

"Don't worry; opportunity will come knocking at your door sooner than you expect," her father told her lightly. "A good detective is always in demand."

"Meaning that I am that?" Nancy demanded, a happy light in her eyes.

Carson Drew nodded and gazed tenderly upon his daughter.

"Meaning that I am mighty proud of you, Nancy. From this day on I intend to turn over my mystery cases to you." His eyes twinkled mischievously. "As a detective, you have me backed completely off the map!"

THE END

THE TED SCOTT FLYING STORIES

By FRANKLIN W, DIXON

Individual Colored Wrappers and Text Illustrations by
WALTER S. ROGERS
Each Volume Complete in Itself.

No subject has so thoroughly caught the imagination of young America as aviation. This series has been inspired by recent daring feats of the air, and is dedicated to Lindberg, Byrd, Chamberlin and other heroes of the skies.

OVER THE OCEAN TO PARIS;
or Ted Scott's daring long distance flight.

RESCUED IN THE CLOUDS;
or, Ted Scott, Hero of the Air.

OVER THE ROCKIES WITH THE AIR MAIL;
or, Ted Scott, Lost in the Wilderness,

FIRST STOP HONOLULU;
or, Ted Scott, over the Pacific.

THE SEARCH FOR THE LOST FLYERS;
or, Ted Scott, Over the West Indies.

SOUTH OF THE RIO GRANDE;
or, Ted Scott, On a Secret Mission.

ACROSS THE PACIFIC;
or, Ted Scott's Hop to Australia.

THE LONE EAGLE OF THE BORDER;
or, Ted Scott and the Diamond Smugglers.

FLYING AGAINST TIME;
or, Breaking the Ocean to Ocean Record.

OVER THE JUNGLE TRAILS;
or, Ted Scott and the Missing Explorers.

LOST AT THE SOUTH POLE;
or, Ted Scott in Blizzard Land.

GROSSET & DUNLAP, *Publishers,* NEW YORK

THE FAMOUS ROVER BOYS SERIES

By ARTHUR M. WINFIELD

(EDWARD STRATEMEYER)

Beautiful Wrappers in Full Color

No stories for boys ever published have attained the tremendous popularity of this famous series. Since the publication of the first volume, The Rover Boys at School, some years ago, over three million copies of these books have been sold. They are well written stories dealing with the Rover boys in a great many different kinds of activities and adventures. Each volume holds something of interest to every adventure loving boy.

A complete list of titles is printed on the opposite page.

THE BLYTHE GIRLS BOOKS

By LAURA LEE HOPE

Author of The Outdoor Girls Series

Illustrated by Thelma Gooch

The Blythe Girls, three in number, were left alone in New York City. Helen, who went in for art and music, kept the little flat uptown, while Margy, just out of business school, obtained a position as secretary and Rose, plain-spoken and business-like, took what she called a "job" in a department store. The experiences of these girls make fascinating reading—life in the great metropolis is thrilling and full of strange adventures and surprises.

THE BLYTHE GIRLS: HELEN, MARGY AND ROSE

THE BLYTHE GIRLS: MARGY'S QUEER INHERITANCE

THE BLYTHE GIRLS: ROSE'S GREAT PROBLEM

THE BLYTHE GIRLS: HELEN'S STRANGE BOARDER

THE BLYTHE GIRLS: THREE ON A VACATION

THE BLYTHE GIRLS: MARGY'S SECRET MISSION

THE BLYTHE GIRLS: ROSE'S ODD DISCOVERY

THE BLYTHE GIRLS: THE DISAPPEARANCE OF HELEN

THE BLYTHE GIRLS: SNOWBOUND IN CAMP

THE BLYTHE GIRLS: MARGY'S MYSTERIOUS VISITOR

GROSSET & DUNLAP *Publishers* NEW YORK

THE OUTDOOR GIRLS SERIES

by LAURA LEE HOPE

Author of The Blythe Girls Books

Every Volume Complete in Itself.

These are the adventures of a group of bright, fun-loving, up-to-date girls who have a common bond in their fondness for outdoor life, camping, travel and adventure. There is excitement and humor in these stories and girls will find in them the kind of pleasant associations that they seek to create among their own friends and chums.

THE OUTDOOR GIRLS OF DEEPDALE
THE OUTDOOR GIRLS AT RAINBOW LAKE
THE OUTDOOR GIRLS IN A MOTOR CAR
THE OUTDOOR GIRLS IN A WINTER CAMP
THE OUTDOOR GIRLS IN FLORIDA
THE OUTDOOR GIRLS AT OCEAN VIEW
THE OUTDOOR GIRLS IN ARMY SERVICE
THE OUTDOOR GIRLS ON PINE ISLAND
THE OUTDOOR GIRLS AT THE HOSTESS HOUSE
THE OUTDOOR GIRLS AT BLUFF POINT
THE OUTDOOR GIRLS AT WILD ROSE LODGE
THE OUTDOOR GIRLS IN THE SADDLE
THE OUTDOOR GIRLS AROUND THE CAMPFIRE
THE OUTDOOR GIRLS ON CAPE COD
THE OUTDOOR GIRLS AT FOAMING FALLS
THE OUTDOOR GIRLS ALONG THE COAST
THE OUTDOOR GIRLS AT SPRING HILL FARM
THE OUTDOOR GIRLS AT NEW MOON RANCH
THE OUTDOOR GIRLS ON A HIKE
THE OUTDOOR GIRLS ON A CANOE TRIP

GROSSET & DUNLAP, *Publishers,* NEW YORK